TSIGA

Wilson Katiyo

TSIGA

Edited by Nigel Watt

Publisher:
Books of Africa Limited
16 Overhill Road
East Dulwich, London
SE22 0PH
United Kingdom

Web site: www.booksofafrica.com
Emails: admin@booksofafrica.com
sales@booksofafrica.com

Copyright© Pauline Dodgson-Katiyo
& Nigel Watt, 2011

ISBN 978-0-9566380-1-4

British Library cataloguing-in-publication data

A catalogue record for this book is available from the British Library.

Printed and bound in the Great Britain by MPG Biddles Ltd, Norfolk, PE30 4LS, United Kingdom.

All rights reserved. No part of this publication may be reproduced, stored in retrieval system, or transmitted in any form or by any means – electronic, mechanical, photocopying, recording or any other, – except for brief quotation in printed reviews, without the prior written permission of the publisher.

INTRODUCTION

The Zimbabwean writer Wilson Katiyo's last novel *Tsiga* was left unfinished and unpublished at the time of his death in 2003. Like his other two novels, **A Son of the Soil** (1976) and **Going to Heaven** (1979), ***Tsiga*** was written when Katiyo was in exile in Europe. This time, though, Katiyo was not escaping from the oppression and racism of Rhodesia as he had been in the 1970s. He had returned to Zimbabwe in 1980 but left again for Europe in 1987, disillusioned by the performance of the post-Independence government. Katiyo lived in Paris and London between 1987 and 2003 and only returned to Zimbabwe for short visits.

Tsiga was written in the 1990s at the same time as Katiyo was working on various film scripts. He was unable to complete the novel after he was diagnosed with cancer. Katiyo's friend and literary executor Nigel Watt edited the *Tsiga* manuscript after Katiyo's death.

Katiyo's first novel **A Son of the Soil**, despite its depiction of racism, was a novel of renewal and hope in a better future. *Tsiga* in contrast is a novel of disillusionment. Like other post-Independent Zimbabwean novels such as Shimmer Chinodya's *Harvest of Thorns* (1989) and Charles Samupindi's *Pawns* (1992), it shows how the ordinary ex-combatant on his return to Zimbabwe after the war becomes a despised member of society unable to benefit from the fruits of independence. It is also unlike *A Son of the Soil* in its departure from the linear narrative of a realist novel. In order to tell his desperate story, Tsiga's narrative makes frequent use of flashbacks, venturing further and further into the past so that the reader gradually comes to understand how Tsiga has reached his current state and why he wants revenge. Katiyo's choice of a non-linear form may have been influenced by his interest in film and scriptwriting.

Tsiga has some characteristics of the picaresque but in this novel, the protagonist is not a young boy journeying through life but a world-weary man who has seen or knows too much and does not expect to have a positive future. Tsiga's story provides a kaleidoscopic view of a contemporary African society. The adventures Tsiga describes introduce a range of topical characters and incidents. Some of them convey the desolate wasteland of a society that has disappointed its people. We are shown the powerful and ambitious nationalist Jerry, politically corrupt and brutal in his domestic life; the philosophical tramp Twoboy who becomes the victim of urban violence and the vulnerable Emma who is too needy herself to provide Tsiga with the reassurance he seeks. Set against this are the traces of what might have been if post-Independence society had followed another path. There is the potential of Tsiga and Mara's love, the happy family scenes when Jerry is absent and the caring nature of the poor woman who takes pity on a thirsty tramp.

Although the country and city depicted in the novel are Katiyo's native Zimbabwe and its capital Harare, some of the place names have been changed. This gives the novel a wider appeal. In postmodern fashion, the story is told in fragments which together form a microcosm of an African society in transition.

Pauline Dodgson-Katiyo
London, 2010

1. THE ROAD

Thanks to that wretched policeman I am now on my way. Lord, what a nose the man has. Must be like carrying a bullfrog on your face. Anyway, were it not for him, I suspect I would still be on that park bench in Springfield Gardens, fast asleep.

The sun won't be up for a while yet but already here I am at the intersection of East Circular and Enterprise Road, with most of the city behind me. All I have to do is follow Enterprise Road until I come to a big blue signpost announcing Capital Farm. To the right, a small winding tarmac road that runs through the farm should lead me to the farmhouse. "No more than fifty kilometres", Emma said. Simple directions, but fifty kilometres is quite a walk by any measure. If my ankle doesn't play up and the farm really is about fifty kilometres from town, I should be there before sunset.

I am not going to be surprised if "Jerry's small country," as she likes to describe Capital Farm, turns out to be further than fifty kilometres. Emma exaggerates. When she was blabbing about her short high-class life with Jerry, she gave me the impression that the farm was virtually on the outskirts of the city. It was only a ten minute drive from the city centre, she repeated a few times. Knowing that there was no farm within ten minutes of the city, I asked her how far Capital Farm actually was. Embarrassed, she stammered and then mumbled that it was fifty kilometres. I don't think Emma has any concept of distance or time. To her, if you were travelling from one end of the horizon to the other, you would be there in no time at all. To her credit though, she always exaggerates the positive. In that sense, one could say she is the ultimate optimist.

No, I don't think I am trying to blame Emma for this long walk ahead of me. On the contrary, I should be grateful to her. Without all the information she gave me, this journey would not be possible. If I have to reproach anybody, it should be myself. I am a damned fool for not taking more coins from her piggybank. I could have taken the lot and she would not have given a damn, that much I know. I was too angry to think straight at the time. Yep, but for that blind rage, I would be getting to Capital Farm in the comfort of a bus seat. Anyhow, this is no time for regrets. I hope Jerry will be at home when I get there. If he is not, there is nothing for it but to wait. I am not going anywhere else before I see the man. A day, a week or a month, I shall wait until I see him. Today being a Saturday, there is a good chance he will be there. Twoboy, who once worked for him, did say that Jerry enjoys being on the farm so much that he spends as much time as he can there, unless he is abroad or travelling elsewhere in the

1. The road

country. Emma confirmed this on more than one occasion. Anyway, my gut feeling is that he is there.

This time, unlike that time I went to his downtown office, there is going to be no young beautiful secretary to tell me Jerry is too busy to see me and that the only way I can communicate with him is by letter. Today, I am not going to let any of his bodyguards humiliate me like they did the last time I tried to see Jerry at his Colney Valley mansion. No bodyguard is going to tell me that Jerry doesn't know me, doesn't want to see me and tell me to take a walk. If I have to fight my way in to see Jerry, I shall.

No need to take offence if Jerry doesn't remember who I am or recognise me. After all, it's more than ten years since we last saw each other. It's not like we were friends. All in all, I think we met only two or three times. Of course, we have both changed since then but I, evidently, more than he. If I am to go by the photographs of him that I see in the newspapers all the time, he has put on a little weight but he still looks his old self. He seems healthy and looks younger than his thirty-eight years. As for me, well, I didn't have this limp when we last met. I know I look dilapidated and older than Jerry himself but all that will change the day I find Mara. But I am not going to blame Jerry if his first impression is that I am a destitute who has come to ask for alms or a job. I can just imagine the scene: he throws me a five, maybe even a ten dollar note, I go down on my knees, head down and break into a praise song. After the song, with hands clasped in a prayer posture, I look up at him and thank him profusely. No, I shall have no time to bullshit like that. In a calm and collected manner, I shall introduce myself. I shall tell him I know what a busy man he is and thank him for granting me an audience. If he invites me into his house, I shall accept but without all the excitement of a simple pauper entering a prince's palace. Inside the house, I shall accept no hospitality. No drink. No food. A seat, yes. On the other hand, if he doesn't ask me in, I shall be just as happy to talk outside. I shall give him Mara's letter to read and ask him if he knows where she is. The rest, we shall take from there.

Mentally, I am not yet as comfortable as I would like to be. In fact, I am feeling anguished but I know that will soon pass. I think I am feeling this way mainly because I don't like being on this deserted road. Today being Saturday, most people won't be going to work and, in any case, it would be a little too early even if it were a weekday. True, a few cars, a couple of cyclists and one or two pedestrians have been up and down the road but it's not the same. Of course, later, it's going to be busy and very lively. Old lorries and run-down trucks full of farm produce will be groaning their way to the city market. The long-distance buses, usually overcrowded, will be roaring in both directions between the city and the east of the country. There will be those who live in the eastern suburbs and work on Saturday mornings on their way to work on foot, on bicycle, motorcycles, in cars and local buses. Despite the noise, the pollution and the inconvenience of walking along a congested road, I still wish there were a few people about and a little more traffic. I am sure the road wouldn't seem so

1. The road

tediously long and straight. Any distraction that would make the journey seem shorter would be welcome. I do cherish my solitude and enjoy my free thoughts but I hate feeling so alone in the world.

Now it occurs to me, this road and my destiny are more closely entwined than I realised before. My twin brother Tom and I were conceived in the city but I know that our dear Ma travelled this road home to Mutoko to give birth to us because she did not want her children to be born in the murky bowels of the city. A week or two after we were born, Tom and I made our first journey ever, in the arms of Ma and Pa, from Mutoko to the city on this old road. Of course, I don't remember it because I was barely two but when Ma died, we all took to this road again.

While I was growing up, before the modern town started eating into the fabric of our traditional society and my extended family, Tom and I used to go up and down this road at least once a month. Every time there was a birth or a marriage in the family, this road took us home and back. At Christmas and other holidays, we always travelled this road. It is amazing that I still have so much feeling for that bygone time. Another past I still live with was ten years ago when I last kissed and embraced Mara. I then took the bus at the Central Bus Station and travelled this way, home, to see Pa who was ill. We were alone when he died in my arms the following day. Seven years later, when the liberation struggle ended, it was this same road that carried me back to the city in triumph. Always this road. I have no doubt that when I die, if I die in the city, I shall be carried along this road to my final resting place. I have travelled on this road as a baby, as a child, as a youth and as a man. This road knows my life. Today, this road takes me to Jerry's farm where fate awaits me.

Now, this is the beginning of Colney Valley. A paradise on earth. people say, our most exclusive suburb. Even from this bypass, I can smell the scent of the jacaranda flowers. Every road, avenue, square and close in the suburb is lined with jacaranda trees. I would bet that there are more jacarandas per square kilometre in Colney Valley than anywhere else in the world. And, at this, the peak of the dry season, the tree is in full bloom. Only top politicians, diplomats and millionaires live here. Jerry's main home is a few blocks down the road. I could not imagine how rich some human beings were until I went to try and see Jerry at his mansion. That was within days of my return to the city at the end of the war. Unfortunately, I was not allowed into the compound nor could I see Jerry. At the time, he had just been appointed Attorney General and he was far too busy to see small fry like me. But from what I later learned from Twoboy, who had once worked as a valet for the great man, I have a very vivid picture of Jerry's main residence. I imagine it to be ultra modern, (in other words plastic) and cluttered. It's stupid, I know, but sometimes I feel like I have actually been inside the house. But more amusing than that is trying to visualise Twoboy garbed in a dark suit and taking orders from his master. I can't picture it without shedding tears of laughter. True, it didn't last very long but it blows my mind that it happened at all. I do miss him.

1. The road

Anyway, as Twoboy described it to me, the residence, set on three acres, is one of the most desirable properties in Colney Valley. Twoboy said he found it hard to imagine any material comforts Jerry and his family missed. He might have exaggerated about the interior of the house and other things but I know for sure that he did not exaggerate about the swimming pool, the tennis courts or the manicured lawns, flower beds and all kinds of tropical fruit trees. Those, I had seen with my own eyes from outside the gate. I did not see what cars were inside the garage but in the carport I was able to see some of Jerry's numerous motor vehicles. Apparently Jerry just loved fast cars. What I did not see, because it was all away from the front gate, were the dog kennels, the chicken coop, the vegetable garden and the horse stables. On four sides, the property was enclosed by a six-foot wall topped by a roll of razor-wire. Four armed guards, working in two shifts, manned the gate and patrolled the compound at all times. A pack of seriously vicious dogs roamed the gardens day and night. Closed circuit television cameras had been fitted all around the house and at various strategic points in the large outdoors. Apart from that, there was also a separate comprehensive burglar alarm system. To top the whole home security system, Jerry kept an automatic pistol under the pillow and slept with one eye open. Some people are lucky. I would have died from the stress of it all.

According to Twoboy, despite his fortune, a brilliant legal career and life under the scent of the jacarandas, Jerry did not seem to enjoy the bliss one would expect.

His marriage was nothing more than a sham. Twoboy also told me that quite often Jerry drank more than was good for him and would invariably end up beating up his wife or driving off to some girlfriend's place. If he had any affection for his two daughters, he showed them none of it. All the servants were terrified of him. The one vice that Twoboy really despised Jerry for was going out with girls less than half his age. His desire for young girls bordered on the perverted. Apparently he suffered from terrible nightmares but Twoboy never discovered what these nightmares were about. He did think they were a serious problem because he saw regular bills from a psychiatrist. Poor Jerry!

This is not bad going. The sun is now rising and Colney Valley is already behind me but not until after Summertown will I be truly out of the city and then the real journey begins. That clear blue sky means it's going to be another scorching day. I must try and cover as much ground as possible before the sun gets too hot. The heat is sure to slow me down. This year the temperatures are really wicked. I shall regret not thinking about taking a bottle of water but how could I have done so with that sadistic Fatnose trying to torture me for no good reason? Anyway, even if I had the water, sooner or later, it would boil in the heat before I could quench my thirst. I shall be all right. There are plenty of villages all along the way. As for food, well, it's better not to think about it. My one real fear is that my leg might play up. It sometimes does when I walk these long distances. If it decides to misbehave, I shall just have to forget about arriving at Capital Farm before

1. The road

nightfall. I don't care even if I get there tomorrow as long as I get there.

A group of children trooping off to school. Strange how they seem to have appeared from nowhere. Surely school doesn't begin this early, especially on a Saturday? Of course, it is Saturday. That too is rather odd. They are in school uniform but no school bags. Probably going on an outing. More girls than boys. Cousin Pete would have loved that. He scored with virtually all the eight girls in our school group. At least he said he did. Seems like only yesterday when Tom, Pete, Manu, myself and the rest of our gang were pushing, shoving and chattering playfully like that on our way to school.

I like the boys' uniform. It is more like what I used to dream of wearing for school. I thought I would look real cool in the black shoes, grey socks, grey flannels, white shirt, blue tie, navy blue blazer and straw hat. The girls look rather drab in their white blouses and brown gym-dresses. Still, they look better than we did in our khaki shirts and shorts. The buggers don't realise how lucky they are.

Stupid kids. They certainly don't have much sense of danger. They shouldn't be walking in the middle of a major road like that. True, there is no traffic but they should be getting into good habits now. Some crazy driver will come flying with his accelerator on the floor and they will scatter in all directions. I would hate to witness any one of them being hurt.

Ah, I have been noticed. All eyes on me. I wonder what they are saying. That tall lanky fellow appears to

Tsiga

dominate everybody. He seems to have them all under his spell. What? Is that really how I am walking? I see. I am staggering all over, like a drunkard. I would say it is a bit exaggerated but what does it matter? It's a good comedy act. He has everybody in stitches; that's what counts. Truth is, he makes me feel like laughing too despite the fact that the fun is at my expense. Even if he doesn't make it in maths or philosophy, the young man should be able to earn a living as an actor. Now that they and I are getting closer, they decide to walk on the other side of the road. Must be afraid of me.

No, my dear friends, believe me, I wouldn't dream of hurting any one of you. No matter what silly or clever little tricks you get up to, in my mind you are the beautiful flowers of life itself. All right, let's try some reasoning. Assuming you are correct that I am drunk and can hardly walk or see where I am going, what harm could I do in this state? No. Now look at who is being stupid. Logic, I should know by now, has nothing to do with how you guys behave. I give up on the idea of trying to reason with you. I like you all very much because, as I said in a different voice, you are the future. Seeing that you are on your way to school, hopefully to learn something, I might as well try to contribute a word or two towards your education. First of all, I want you to know that things are not always what they seem to be. To explain what I mean, let me tell you a personal tale.

When I was about eight, my hero was Uncle Thomas, my father's brother. He was big. He was strong and he was fast. But best of all, my uncle was smart. I could never have a question to which he did not have the

1. The road

answer. I liked spending time with him because he taught me a lot of things in a nice way. He was patient and was always there for me. And, oh, he could be funny too.

One day, I took a stroll to his house because I wanted him to take me rock climbing. When I got there, he wasn't home. So I sat outside his door and waited for him. Soon enough, I spotted him coming up the road. Delighted that he was home, I raced to meet him but immediately I noticed that he wasn't walking the way he normally did. Something was wrong. He was meandering all over the road and several times I thought he was going to fall. He nearly bumped into an elderly couple who laughed and accused him of being drunk. I couldn't believe it because I had never seen my uncle drunk before. As I got closer to him, more people passing by uttered some unpleasant remarks and made fun of Uncle Thomas. I tried talking to him but it did no good. He was sweating and could hardly keep his eyes open. He wasn't behaving in a happy and silly way like I had seen drunk people do. I put my arm around his waist and helped him home but, with Uncle Thomas being so big, it wasn't easy. We struggled home and eventually I managed to get him into the house and on to his bed. He was so drunk he didn't seem to even know where he was or who I was, let alone utter one audible word. I was pretty upset to see him like that. I didn't even know that he drank. I sat by his bedside until he fell asleep. Disappointed that we couldn't go climbing, I slowly walked home.

Tsiga

When I got home, Pa could see something was wrong. He tried to cheer me up and asked me what the matter was but I didn't want him to know that Uncle Thomas was drunk. But as usual, in the end, I had to tell the truth. Pa was shocked. He told me that Uncle Thomas never touched alcohol. I told him to go and see for himself if he didn't believe me. In a panic, Pa rushed to his brother's house. He was away a long time. When he came back, tears were streaming down his face. It was frightening. He sat me on his lap and told me Uncle Thomas had died of something called a brain haemorrhage. Right away, I knew somehow it was my fault. Oh boy, did I cry. I cried my eyes out. I couldn't believe that I would never talk or go out with my uncle again. If I had gone home quickly and told Pa everything, my uncle could have been taken to hospital earlier and might have survived. Pa tried to reassure me that it wasn't my fault but even today I don't feel so sure.

From my appearance, I bet most of you believe I must be at least a hundred years old. Call me a liar if you like but in reality I am just twenty-seven. No, I won't blame you if you think I came out of my mother's womb wearing this long hair, wild beard, my tattered blue jacket, this filthy yellow shirt, my soiled grey trousers and this worn out cheap pair of shoes. I agree with you that I probably look like somebody who has never had a bath since the day he was born. In your heart you know this isn't so. In my small ears, buried under this dirty bush of black hair, I can hear your derisive laughter when I tell you that I have a first class degree in physics.

1. The road

Some of you will be so scandalised that you will think I should be in a mental hospital. I can hear you asking why I don't have a job if I am that well qualified. Well, the short answer to the question is that I don't know how to live a life without love. Without love to both give and receive, my life is not worth living. You see, with Mara, it's not just why or how we are in love, it's because of what we know. Now, be careful how you interpret this. I am not talking about sex. I mean love. The only love I have ever found is in the heart of a young woman named Mara. You see, unless I find her, my life is doomed. No, clearly you don't understand. I am trying to tell you that Mara is the only commitment I have in life. Nothing, not even poverty, is going to stand in the way of my love for her. Before you rush to your own conclusions about my foolishness and all that, let me tell you that I regret nothing. Nothing, except that despite three years of searching, I have still not found Mara. If you want to understand what I am saying, forget about your school class this morning and come with me all the way to Capital Farm. I shall tell you my whole story with Mara on the way.

Before we part, dear friends, let's get one or two things right. Please let me assure you that I am not drunk. I have a problem with my leg. Shrapnel. Right at my ankle. I call it my souvenir from the liberation struggle. If you were more observant, you would have noticed that I was limping, not staggering. From time to time, I enjoy a good drink but I can't stand the smell of alcohol any time before a midday meal. And that's the truth. Now that we have cleared this up, it's time to

Tsiga

bid each other farewell. Goodbye, my young friends. Go your ways as I take mine. Love, by the way, can only be found in the living.

2. FATNOSE

Nearly out of Summertown. Now, there is somebody who is drunk and if he is not, then he must be totally crazy. Even if this was his damn private road, that's no way to ride a bicycle. Sure, it's very impressive riding at that speed with his hands off the handlebar and zigzagging all over the road like that but sooner than later, it will all end in grief. A man of his age ought to be ashamed to be skylarking like a schoolboy. At that speed, if he makes one mistake, he will end up in a wheelchair or dead. And then we are all expected to feel sorry. Big deal. The idiot coming straight for me! Bastard! After frightening the life out of me, he has the cheek to look back and smile at me. All I say is shame on you. If you wanted me in the ditch, well, too bad I am not in it. If you meant to run me over, I am sorry, better luck next time.

Bloody moron! Imagine a lunatic like him driving a car. Aah! The skylark is grounded. He bloody well deserves it. For once, I get instant justice. I hope the fool has broken a leg or something. That would teach him not to menace innocent souls like me. Thought he was so good he could even ride without looking where he was going. Well, there he is and can't even get up. What? Help him after his arrogant antics? Oh, no. I hope he is still smiling through all that moaning and groaning. I can't think why he tried to hassle me. Some people I shall never understand. I can't decide whether he is worse or better than that policeman Fatnose.

One day I might forget all about Fatnose but it will take the rest of my days to forget that monster of a nose with its massive nostrils. I know he didn't choose to be born with such a nose but that doesn't mean I have to pretend it's pretty. Life must be tough for him. It is no wonder the man has a chip on his shoulder.

Now it all seems so remote but only a couple of hours ago, Fatnose was giving me hell. That kind of experience usually comes only out of the cinema. There I was deep in a dreamless sleep on the bench when he came along and, without any kind of warning, grabbed me by the lapels of my jacket and pulled me up. Startled and confused, I simply assumed that I was being mugged. After all it was happening hundreds of times a day in our city. Naturally, knowing what had happened to Twoboy last week, I was terrified. My number is up, I kept on thinking. An image of Twoboy struggling for his life flashed through my mind. I was really bewildered. The next instant, Jerry's face, with its sardonic smile, forced itself into my mind. That must have been because I thought he might have organised this attack. I wanted to cry. I felt intensely bitter to think he had outwitted me.

2. Fatnose

Up on my feet, in the thin morning light, the first thing I noticed about my assailant was that he was a bulky figure in a special constable's uniform and had a baton in the other hand. My fear of being robbed and then murdered receded. I wasn't being mugged after all. Police officers, even the poorly paid and unarmed special constables, are not supposed to attack members of the public for no good reason. Fatnose jerked me up again so close to his face that I ended up seeing nothing except the two tunnels of nose and the small mouth which seemed to have frozen open. I wanted to laugh but I knew it would be suicide. I waited for him to head-butt me or say something but for some reason he just stood there, exhaling his stale breath down my face. I did wonder if he was trying to gas me to death with his foul breath. I felt like a hapless prey under the claws of its predator.

Despite all the turmoil going on inside me, I instinctively thought it best to remain calm and submissive under the grip of his strong hand. I didn't want to provoke him in any way. In any case, there was nothing much I could have done against him at that moment. I thought about the Colt .45 tucked at the back of my trousers. The safety catch was on. I feared that if I made one false move, Fatnose would wrench my head off my body. Now, I thought, even our police officers have joined in on the violence against the homeless. Unless, of course, this gorilla was just pretending to be a special constable. I took a deep breath and sighed. His grip eased and he gave me a little shove but he did not let go of my jacket. It was only then that I could just make out a pair of small bloodshot eyes embedded deep in his head under the cap. From that moment, I started thinking of Fatnose as more of a beast than a man. Of course, I wanted to ask him what the whole fuss was about but I didn't dare. If there was going to be any talking, Fatnose had to break the silence. It really was a bizarre scene. Instinctively, I kept my senses alert for any possible movement of the baton. I figured that by the time he raised it up and then brought it down on my head or anywhere else on my person, it was possible to kick him in the groin and then pull the gun on him. If he turned brutal, I was ready to shoot him. After taking the gun from Emma's house, I had promised myself that I would never use it unless I had to. I still preferred the situation to be resolved peacefully, if at all possible, but it wasn't up to me. Meanwhile, I waited for him to make the next move.

After what seemed like ages, Fatnose stated, in an astonishingly feminine voice, that I was breaking the law by sleeping in a public place. I didn't respond partly because it wasn't a question and partly because I was still recovering from the surprising sound of his very high voice. I think Fatnose took my silence as a gesture of insolence. Desperately trying to sound harsh, he asked me if his statement was not true. Feigning politeness and humility, I told him that I hadn't realised it was an offence. His little voice rising to anger, he called me a bloody liar. He claimed that he knew me very well and that I was always in trouble with the police for sleeping in public places. We both knew he was lying. Although I was getting quite irritated, I remai-

2. Fatnose

ned silent, reminding myself that it was important for me to weather this storm – and weather it as soon as possible without violence. For his sake rather than mine, I hoped that he was not going to try and arrest me. I was not prepared to be arrested for vagrancy and to end up being charged with "the illegal possession of a dangerous weapon". A more important reason was that nobody was going to interfere with my date with Jerry.

"You are a beggar, aren't you?" he accused me.

I felt like I had suddenly been flipped upside down and it hurt.

"No, sir," I replied, sounding less sarcastic than I intended to be.

"You are a tramp and a liar!" he shouted like a trumpeting baby elephant.

"No, sir," I repeated, struggling to maintain my cool.

"'No, sir, no sir,'" he mimicked. "You think I am a bloody idiot! You think you can make a fool out of me, eh?" he cried, shaking me violently by the lapels of my coat. I wished his bear's body was as tiny as his voice.

"You are lucky. I feel sorry for you. This time I will let you go but next time I see you sleeping here or any other public place, I will make sure you go to prison for a long time, do you understand?"

I nodded.

"I said do you fucking understand?" he screamed.

"Yes, officer," I affirmed, pretending to be meek.

"Now get out of here before I change my mind," he cried, as he finally loosened his grip. He pushed me backwards and I stumbled. Fortunately I did not fall.

"Out! Out! Out!" he shooed me off like a stray dog.

Retreating, I pleaded with him to let me take my bag which was on the bench but Fatnose was in no mood to listen. His splendid nose quivering with rage, he strode towards me, brandishing his baton and calling me every dirty name that came into his head. I thought of threatening him with my gun but I realised it would cause more problems for me than the bag was worth. I could see the situation easily getting out of hand. I decided the bag wasn't worth the trouble. I turned and started walking towards the nearest gate out of Springfield Park. I felt foolish walking away from my bag like that. Just before I got to the gate, I remembered that Mara's letter was in the bag. I didn't want to go and see Jerry without it. I didn't care a damn about anything else in that bag but I was not going anywhere without that letter. I turned round and walked back towards the bench. I could think of no good reason why Fatnose would hang around there after I had left but, just in case, I took the safety catch off the Colt and kept it handy in the hip of my trousers. If my bag was missing from the bench, I felt I had no choice but to go the police station and report it stolen. I would have simply described my encounter with Fatnose. Of course, I would not have been so foolish as to walk into the police station with the pistol. I would have hidden it in any one of a thousand secluded places in Springfield Park. Very soon, I discovered how mistaken I was.

There, on the bench, I found Fatnose horizontal, with his cap over his face. My bag was his pillow. I couldn't suppress a hearty chuckle. That startled him.

2. Fatnose

When he saw me, he jumped up and his cap fell to the ground. I thought, just for an instant, he looked sheepish. Before he could say a word, I told him I merely wanted to take my bag and leave. He picked up his cap and motioned me to take the bag. I sensed no hint of animosity. Grateful that I could retrieve my bag with no complications, I walked over to the bench but just as I was lifting it up, Fatnose grabbed me by the wrist and twisted it. I thought, oh no, here we go again.

"What the hell did I tell you just before you left?" he demanded, shaking with emotion.

"Please let me just take my bag and go," I begged him.

"I told you I would arrest you, didn't I?"

My patience was running thin. I was no longer in the mood for that kind of shit but I decided to ask him to be reasonable one more time.

"Please, officer," I said, pleading, "the sooner you let me take my bag, the sooner you can continue with your rest. So, please..."

I had asked for it! I don't know how he did it but in a flash, he had released me from his grip and given me a mighty backhand slap across my face which sent me reeling to the ground.

"Rest? What are you talking about? Tell me, what rest are you talking about?"

I was in shock. I wiped blood from the corner of my mouth and looked at my hand. As far as I was concerned, that was it. Fatnose had crossed the line. In a remote region of my mind, I heard him yelling obscenities but I was no longer afraid of him or the consequences of my actions. My mind was in a spin but I knew what I was going to do next. Seething, I remained on the ground, watching him like a hawk. He started walking over to me. I was pleased that as a special constable, Fatnose had no gun. Calmly, I pulled out the pistol and aimed it at his flabby nose. When he saw the lethal end of the .45, I thought he was going to have a heart attack. I cocked the pistol and he started quaking. I didn't say a word but with his hands up in the air, slowly he began to move backwards. I stood up. I ordered him to stop and he did. Scared, he looked even more ugly. He pleaded with me to take my bag and leave before I did something I might regret. I thanked him for his suggestion but reminded him that it was he who, instead of letting me take my bag and go, had just assaulted me. I had no idea of what he was going to say next but I told him to keep his mouth shut. We stared at each other in silence for a while. I was trying to work out an effective way of getting rid of him as I didn't want the police mounting a manhunt after I had left him. A solid idea was coming into my head.

In a docile voice, he asked me what I was going to do with him. I informed him it was in his best interest to co-operate fully. I told him I had nothing to lose and had no qualms about killing him and I think at the time I meant it. I wasn't a good shot but I didn't think I could miss his nose. He saw sense in what I was saying and agreed to do as I instructed. I asked Fatnose to walk right up to me with his hands behind his head. When he was close enough I poked the cold steel of the Colt

2. Fatnose

right on his temple. Apart from sweating profusely, Fatnose was pissing in his trousers. With his assistance, I easily handcuffed the big man's hands behind him. It was my turn to enjoy myself. I asked Fatnose if he liked jazz. He told me he couldn't say because he didn't really know much about it. He was now very polite. Cordially, I told him that basically it was all about creativity and improvisation.

    I hadn't thought out what I was going to do with him but my game plan was to find a way of making sure Fatnose caused me no further problems, especially now that he knew I had a gun. My little story to him was that I was broke and I hadn't had sex for years. This part of it was true. I asked him, as a police officer, if he could use his authority and persuade a prostitute in the nearby red-light district of Cheapside to have sex with me. With an enthusiasm that surprised me, he told me that it would be no problem because he knew several attractive girls who owed him favours in the area. He told me I could have more than one if I felt like it. He assured me that I was going to enjoy myself to my heart's content but he also wanted me to promise not to hurt him. My response was that it all depended on him. If he was going to try and be smart with me, he might get hurt, I warned him. I thought his baton was an unnecessary baggage and so we left it on the bench. He said he could always come back for it after our little adventure. With my slight limp, I thought we would look more natural if he had my bag slung over his broad shoulder. He raised no objections. Finally, I warned him not to look back, make any sudden movements or try any monkey business. It seemed like he understood what I meant all right. Our agreements concluded, we set off for Cheapside which was no more than a kilometre from where we were in Springfield Park. Fatnose walked a pace or so ahead of me.

As soon as we started walking, Fatnose offered me the princely sum of six dollars and seventy-five cents, which was all the cash he had, in return for his freedom. I pretended to consider the offer seriously but in the end, I declined it. Fatnose said I should have it anyway even though I was not going to release him. Again, I refused the money and he appeared somewhat surprised by that. I told him all I wanted was for him to arrange for me to have the company of a young lady and nothing more. After my visit to the brothel, he and I would go our separate ways.

For a while, I couldn't think of anything to say to my new friend. Eventually, I decided to beguile time by getting to know my partner a little better. Fatnose was thirty-two years old and had been a police officer for nine years. He had been married to a schoolteacher but, unhappily, she had left him for a more prosperous man, a teller in a bank. He cited constant financial pressures as the main reason for the break-up of their marriage. Custody of their two little girls had been granted to the ex-wife. Despite the fact that virtually his whole salary went to support the kids, Fatnose hardly saw his children. According to him, they were extremely bright and were doing very well in school. He was still in love with his wife and missed the girls very much but he admitted he had nothing to offer them. No one could

2. Fatnose

fail to be moved by such a sad story. I muttered my regrets and some words of sympathy for his situation. I told him I believed police officers ought to be paid more because they work very hard, day and night.

Our conversation became more pleasant as we strolled out of the dim lights of Springfield Park and into the sleepy streets of Cheapside. Anybody who might have seen us would have been forgiven for thinking we were two good old friends. Fortunately for me, neither the few pedestrians we saw nor the drivers who passed by came close enough to us for Fatnose to chance some escape. I asked Fatnose about his career. He was more forthcoming than I had anticipated. Since he was a small boy, he had always wanted to be a policeman. So it was a great day when he eventually became one. He enjoyed the training and was the best cadet in his group. He worked hard and soon rose through the ranks, ending up with the rank of inspector. Inevitably, some of his fellow officers became jealous. They tried all kinds of dirty tricks to blacken his name but got nowhere. Eventually, they framed him for taking kickbacks. While those false allegations were being investigated, his seniors had been forced to put him on the beat.

I was absorbed in his intriguing story when, suddenly, Fatnose tried to trip me by kicking me on the shinbone of my bad leg. Unfortunately for him, he missed. I shoved the pistol into his ribs and told him I would pump every bullet out of the gun into him if he tried another stupid move like that. I warned him that if he dared even to cough, there was to be no second warning. He tried to tell me it had all been an accident but, angrily, I told him to shut up and walk on in front of me. He was really terrified. We walked the rest of the way to the beginning of the red-light area without a word to each other. By then, I knew exactly what I was going to do with Fatnose.

When we got to the edge of the red-light district, I ordered him to turn into a small isolated side street. In a frightened voice, he asked me what I was going to do with him. I told him to shut up because he would soon find out. He didn't like the street because, besides being rather isolated, it was very dark. We came to a lamp-post where the bulb was broken and I ordered Fatnose to stop. With the gun firmly stuck at his spine, I undid his belt, unzipped his trousers and managed to have them down to his ankles. He was reluctant when I told him to sit on the ground but when the Colt invited him there was no hesitation. Cautious as I needed to be, it took some doing but I was able to remove his shoes and socks before pulling off his soiled trousers and underwear. Using his tie, I secured his feet with the lamp-post between his legs before I began the more dangerous task of transferring the handcuffs from his hands to his feet. When Fatnose finally realised that I was going to leave him there, I think he wished I had shot him instead. After gathering every item of his clothing, with a smile, I wished him all the best for the future and bade him farewell. A few metres up the road, I deposited everything including the keys to the handcuffs in a rubbish bin. I am sure he must have

2. Fatnose

proved quite a sight for the locals before his fellow officers arrived.

I am glad Fatnose and I are quits, otherwise I would still be feeling very bitter about the way he treated me. I would be calling him a heartless bastard just for trying to do his job in the best way he knew how. Just doing his job! What the hell was he doing in Springfield Park at four o'clock in the morning anyway? He should have been out there, in the streets, patrolling or catching real criminals instead of tormenting a harmless creature like me in a public park. The trouble is that some of these so-called law enforcement officers know nothing about the law, let alone the spirit of the law. Did Fatnose really believe that I had left a comfortable bed somewhere in the city to come out and spend the night in the park just to break the law? I don't understand how a self-respecting person can treat another human being the way he treated me. He didn't have to be an intelligent policeman to be able to decide to caution me for such a minor offence and then let me go or simply arrest me if he so wished. Fatnose seems to me like one of those thugs who join the police force for the authority it gives them over ordinary people. Once in uniform, they enjoy the power and forget about upholding the law. When they are not abusing authority, they like flaunting it. I can't help thinking that if he were not a policeman he would be in prison.

I have to say I am glad he didn't try to arrest me. It would have been a real disaster if he had tried to. If he had succeeded, I would have lost my gun and the trip to Jerry's would have been off indefinitely. I am not sure I would have been able to live with that. If he had forced me into shooting him, I think I would have eventually given myself up to the police but not before the business with Jerry. I would rather be punished for killing Fatnose than for murdering Jerry.

Now that I can think more clearly about it, I don't think Fatnose was on patrol when he found me in Springfield Park. Those little red eyes pleading with me not to leave him naked and cuffed to the lamp-post must have meant he was very tired. Working the night beat is tough. I strongly suspect that the bench is his regular nook for a short snooze. Let's say this morning he arrives and finds an intruder. He is tired and gets pissed off. I would be mad too if I found an invader on what I considered my territory at a time I needed it most. No wonder I found him sleeping like a baby and snoring when I went back for my bag. This has to be the only explanation. To the best of my knowledge, Springfield Park has never been notorious for any kind of crime. Not even as a haven for the homeless. It warrants no attention from the police. No, to suggest that Fatnose's beat includes the secluded parts of the park is stretching reality too far. Fatnose had no other business in the park except to sleep. Enough of the Fatnose, the lost soul. Time to think about what lies ahead. After Capital Farm, it might be a good idea to get myself arrested and go to prison for a while. It would be the best way of keeping out of serious trouble.

A shame my friend Fatnose knows I have got a gun otherwise I would have given him the chance of

2. Fatnose

getting the credit for arresting and sending me to jail. Of course, if I didn't have the gun, I wouldn't have been able to leave him in Cheapside. The scenario would be different. Just finding me on that bench a second time so soon after our first meeting would really incense him. I am sure he is dying to improve his arrest record. Second time around he would oblige and arrest me for vagrancy. I would do everything possible to avoid his violence but once inside the police station, I would poke fun at him and his nose in front of witnesses. This and a bit of name calling would be sufficient for Fatnose to try and pile as many minor charges as possible against me. In court, I would plead not guilty. That would work against me. I would be arrogant and abusive to both the prosecutor and the magistrate. They would have to charge me with contempt of court. I would definitely be found guilty and sent to prison. The question of a fine wouldn't arise since I don't have a cent to my name. A couple of months or a maximum of a year would be just fine with me. After the sentence, I would give Fatnose a huge grin. That would baffle the buffoon. But, as it is, he may be thick but perhaps he might just put two and two together and link me to Jerry's impending doom.

No. I will go back to Southville and break some shop window or assault a policeman or do something equally senseless. Mustn't forget to hide my gun before that. If there is a chance of escaping a custodial sentence or having only a short prison sentence, I could always insult the magistrate and be further charged with contempt. Ideally, it would be great to live off

Tsiga

the taxpayer for three or so months. I wouldn't have to worry about food. It's not my idea of freedom to have to sleep in a van or under the open sky on many cold and interminable nights.

I haven't been out of the city for donkey's years. I should go out into the country more often because, at heart, I am a country boy. Out here, I feel myself. I've left the stress of the city behind. My body is already beginning to relax. In this natural environment, my senses are always sharp and taut. The silence and the sounds of the wild seem to permeate into my body and my mind and soothe my whole person. With my eyes on the horizon, not needing to look where I am going, I get some perspective of my place in the universal arrangement of things. As Mara used to say, living in the city is such a waste. But for her, I would really be at peace. On some of our long walks, Mara and I used to dream about going to live a country life on our own small farm, far, far away from any town. We would grow our own food and try to live as naturally as possible. Once in a while, we would go into town for a day or two to fetch necessities, buy books and go to the cinema. All we wanted was to enjoy a simple lifestyle and not look for fortune or fame. Neither of us had any objections to living in the fast lane or making millions on the stock exchange while lying in bed at home. But that was not how we wanted to live our lives. God knows how much I miss that woman wherever she is. It hurts to remember those happy carefree days.

2. Fatnose

No, I don't think all the answers lie beyond that great mysterious blue sky. Nor do I believe they are all to be found under the carpet of those hauntingly beautiful yellow leaves or the dead savannah below them. It is the sun that gives those naked buds, in shades of red, pink, orange and yellow, the splendour to signal a new season, a new life. For today, I shall believe that it is the radiance of the sun that keeps telling me that Mara is alive and is somewhere close by. How do I know that the answers to my questions are not in the syllables of the bird songs I hear? If Mara is alive, Jerry's miserable life shall be spared. I shall recall this just as I remember that the cry of that baby baboon is to remind me that I am not alone. And here comes a bus, tearing down like a raging beast, bellowing a thick black cloud of diesel fumes.

3. EMMA

It was already late afternoon when I woke up last Monday. For a long time, I lay on the floor trying to work out some things in my head. I found myself watching the rays of the setting sun which were penetrating the cracks in the body of the van. There, on the opposite wall, the rays painted what appeared to me to be an image of Twoboy bleeding to death. The choking anguish which I had felt since his death returned. I don't think I knew exactly what for but I felt this strong urge to pray. It was strange because I had never prayed before. After thinking about it, I dismissed the idea as futile. Not even a one-off fervent supplication from a heathen like me would bring him back. Wherever it was, Twoboy's soul didn't need anybody's prayer. I began to feel certain that Twoboy was as happy where he was as he had been when he was alive. The more I thought about it, the less reason I saw why he would transform his character and personality after departing this life. I came to the conclusion that, if at all, I was probably more in need of his prayers and sympathy than he needed mine. Here I was, so hungry I could hardly get out of bed, thinking there might be a God. I had eaten almost nothing since his death last Wednesday. Staying in bed for almost two days after burying Twoboy hadn't done me much good. I was drained, both physically and emotionally. I realised that, mentally too, my grip on reality was getting loose. I could no longer control it but my mind was in and out of a trance. I decided it was time to pull myself together. It was a long while before I felt strong enough to get out of bed. There was not a morsel of anything to eat in the van. I would go to the shops and buy a can of corned beef or a tin of sardines, bread and some beer. After eating, I should feel uplifted and might start thinking straight about what I was going to do next.

The centre of Southville was swarming with people. It was the rush hour. Although the sun had gone down, there was still some daylight. As I approached the shopping centre, my mind was elsewhere. I didn't notice the group of six youths who had surrounded me until one of them grabbed my hand and started shepherding me towards an alley at the back of the local bank. A second member of the gang poked what I assumed to be a knife into the side of my belly and warned me that if I so much as coughed, he was going to rip my guts out. I knew he meant it. I wasn't going to try and resist in any way. I was feeling too lethargic to be frightened. If they were going to kill me, I wanted to die in as little agony as possible. Without addressing the question to any one of them in particular, I asked why they couldn't rob the bank for some serious money rather than go to all the bother for the few

3. Emma

cents I had. A third member of the gang shook me by the collar of my coat and told me to shut up. I don't know why but I looked up at the clear evening sky and thought: they killed Twoboy in the morning and now they are about to kill me in the evening. I wondered if there was any symbolism in that.

Without any warning, I was suddenly pressed against a wall and ordered to empty all my pockets. There was nothing in my pockets except three dollars and fifty cents which I handed over. A couple who might have been a husband and wife passed by, saw what was happening and hurried away. I was ordered to remove my shoes and smelly socks. I had to shake the socks to prove there was no money hidden there. The wretch who had grabbed my hand right at the start of the nightmare carefully went through each and every pocket of my clothing but he found nothing. He then took a step back and nodded to the one who had pushed the flick-knife on to my stomach. It's odd that even today I cannot recall the exact details of the ordeal. Everything happened in a flash. The thirty seconds or so when the knife went up and came down seemed interminable. I realised it was over when I found myself crouched, hugging myself and weeping like a desolate urchin. When I noticed that my jacket, shirt and trousers had been ripped to shreds, I suddenly started shivering uncontrollably. I became so panicky that for a few moments I couldn't be certain where I was. It took me a while to recover. Still crouched against the wall, I found myself admiring the dexterity of the boy who had done so much damage to my clothes but somehow had left me with not even a tiny scratch. I felt so humiliated I wished I had been killed. Somehow, I felt I was to blame for it all but I also knew that if I had made even a minor gesture of resistance, the boy with the knife would have killed me without a second thought. Eventually, I stood up and was surprised to discover the evening had grown very dark. I started walking towards the police station to report the incident. I didn't feel faint any more. I was no longer hungry but both humiliation and anger were still burning on my face.

When I came out of the dark alley into the bright streetlights of the shopping centre, it seemed everybody around was staring at me. I felt so ashamed walking there in my tattered clothes. I thought I should just go straight back to the van and forget all about reporting the matter to the police but I needed someone to listen to my story. I was aware of the fact that there was very little the police could do for me but I wanted to go on record. So I pressed on towards the police station. Fortunately, I spotted two police officers strolling and chatting on the other side of the street. Relieved, I rushed over to them, nearly getting run over by a car in the process. Even before I could open my mouth, they seemed to be already laughing and mocking me with their eyes. They wouldn't listen to a word I tried to say until after they had interrogated me. They wanted to know my name, my date of birth, where I had been born, my address in Southville, what I did for a living. They still wouldn't let me speak about the mugging until I told them that both my parents were dead, I had no sister, my brother had been killed during the war, I

3. Emma

had neither a wife nor children. They asked me a lot of other irrelevant questions and seemed to have forgotten that I had come to them to report something. Each answer I gave was punctuated by either a cynical comment or some snide remark.

"Now, what seems to be the problem?" the shorter of the two finally asked.

Briefly, I explained what had taken place.

"How much did they take from you?"

When I told them I had been robbed of three dollars and fifty cents, they laughed.

"What, exactly, are you expecting us to do about this?" asked the shorter policeman.

"I am reporting this more for the violence I was subjected to than for the money. You can see what they have done to my clothes. I had a friend killed last week. Who knows, it might even be the same gang."

"Indeed, who knows, it might not even be the same gang," retorted the shorter officer in the same cynical voice.

"Show me where it hurts and I shall radio for an ambulance right away," said the officer, getting a little excited.

"You told us you are unemployed. Isn't that right? Would you like to tell us where you got the three dollars and fifty cents from?" the taller partner demanded accusingly. They were like two dogs facing a cornered quarry.

"If you need new clothes, just go to the Red Cross or the Oxfam office and they will give you some. Free," the shorter officer said, raising his voice.

Anger, murderous anger, welled inside me. Before I started walking away, I gave the short policeman a good hard stare. Slowly, his hand moved to rest on the Colt in his gun belt. Something clicked in the roof of my head. A painful smile contorted my face as I remembered that I had my own Colt.45 at 434 Sunningdale Road. Slowly, I walked away from the two policemen. I decided to go to Emma's to get my gun. But before that, I wanted to go to the van and have a change of clothes. I wasn't going to let her see me in those shredded clothes. In fact, I didn't want Emma to know anything about the mugging. As I walked to the van, I wondered how I could have so completely forgotten about the Colt. My first thought was that if I had remembered it before, there was a chance Twoboy might still be alive. Although I was pleased that I was going to be able to protect myself, I was apprehensive about walking the streets at that time of the night.

The pistol had been issued to me the day I was appointed base commander at Camp 7 during the war. I remember that my first reaction was one of disappointment with the gun because it was soiled and looked antiquated. During the early part of the war, I had lots of problems with it and hardly ever used it. But later, after it had received the attentions of a brilliant young comrade called Mohamed, I discovered that it was very effective. On two separate occasions, if I had not had that gun, I would have been killed. I began to rely on it and carried it all the time until the war ended. When I was demobilised, I surrendered all my other weapons but, with the connivance of my commanding

3. Emma

officer, I retained the Colt. Since it was an outdated model, the army didn't have much use for it. I wanted it purely for sentimental reasons and as a souvenir. Although my commander urged me to get a licence for it, I thought, hell, why go through all the bother for a mere memento. I took it home and lovingly cleaned and oiled it before putting it away. Actually, I hid it because it was loaded and I didn't want Emma or any of her visitors messing around with it. I then completely forgot all about it until I saw the policeman's Colt. Deciding that from then on I was going to carry a gun was one thing but going to Emma's to collect it was quite another.

To be honest, if it wasn't for the fact that I was desperate to have the gun, I would probably not have even thought about her. The last time I saw Emma, I promised myself that I never wanted to see her again. That time just after the war I had been overwhelmed by the thought that both Mara and Tom might be dead. As I went up to the familiar house, I felt so happy. A couple of old cars were parked outside. The lights in the whole house were on. I could hear voices, laughter and some jazz music. It was obvious that there was some sort of party going on. I knocked on the front door. Instead of Tom or Emma, a lady clutching a beer bottle opened the door. I asked her if Tom or Emma was still living there.

"Come on in, sweetheart," she said, gesturing me in, "You don't need any excuse to be here."

I walked in past her. There were about twenty people or so. Some were sitting down and others were standing about but everybody had a drink. I looked around for Tom or Emma but I couldn't see either. The room reeked of stale tobacco, sweat and cheap perfume.

"My name is Bea. What can I get you to drink, sweetheart?" she asked trying to sound sexy.

"Do you know where Tom or Emma is?"

"Yeah, Emma is my best friend. You don't want me but you want Emma, right?"

"Right."

"All right. Emma will come. But I asked you if you want a drink."

"Okay, I will have a beer. Thanks."

"Give me twenty-four bucks."

"Sorry?"

I thought I hadn't heard her right.

"Twenty-four bucks, lover boy."

"For one beer. You must be joking."

I heard a threatening male voice from behind me say, "She is not. You ordered two beers. Yeah, twelve dollars each. Pay up, man."

He was as tall as I was but he was stockier. It was evident that his face had been a battleground many times. Scars. Knife wounds. One damaged eye. I did fancy my chances with him but would the rest of the people stand by and let it be? I was sober. I was still fit. I had the gun in the inside pocket of my jacket. For all I knew this was still my brother's house.

"Did you hear what I said? Pay up, motherfucker!" He had done it. Before he knew what was happening, he was on the floor. I kicked him in the face and ordered him to remain down. The women started screaming.

3. Emma

Another guy flicked a knife. He found himself facing the barrel of my small gun. People started running out. That was when I saw Emma standing in the doorway leading to the kitchen. She walked towards me, tears streaming down her face.

"Tell your remaining friends to go home because we need to talk."

She didn't have to say or do anything. They had heard me. They all hurried out and left me alone with her.

"Can I hug you?" she asked, her voice full of fear.

I put my gun in my pocket and went to embrace her.

"Life has been very hard, Tsiga. I had to do something. I had to survive," she cried.

"I know. I know. Where is Tom?" I asked as I disengaged.

"I don't know. I thought you were together."

I felt weak in the knees and slumped on the sofa. She went to the kitchen and brought me a beer.

"Emma, please sit down. . . When did you last see Tom?"

"The day he left for your father's funeral. When neither of you came back, maybe a week after he left, I checked every hospital for either of you. I checked with every police station. I went to Mutoko but the village had been destroyed, burnt down by the army. I checked and re-checked the hospitals and police-stations but all in vain. Eventually, I accepted that you might have decided to go and join the liberation struggle."

"I was forced to. Maybe he too was forced to."

"I am sorry that you had to arrive and find....."

"Don't worry about that. When did you last see Mara?"

"Well, for weeks after you disappeared, she came looking for you and asking if I had news either from you or from Tom. After some weeks, she stopped coming."

My mind was in turmoil. All kinds of thoughts were racing through my mind. Emma started preparing some food and cleaning up the house. Some of her customers kept on turning up but she sent them away. I offered to leave but she wouldn't hear of it.

After dinner, both Emma and I felt more relaxed and talked. She really didn't know anything more about my brother than what she had already told me. But she was very eager to impress on me that she had done everything she could to find out what had happened to both Tom and me. I agreed with her that it was most likely that like me, Tom might have had to join the Liberation Front Army.

We also agreed that if he were alive, he would be home in a matter of days. I told her that there were still thousands of other comrades who had been ordered to remain out of the country by the High Command because it didn't want everybody to come back until the Front had taken over complete control. While I was talking to Emma, many thoughts were going through my mind. The most important decision I made was that I was not going to do anything like looking for a job or settling down until I had found both Tom and Mara. If they were both dead, I wanted to know. My demobilisation pay, which I was yet to receive, wasn't much but

3. Emma

I was going to stretch it as far as possible. Hopefully, I would find out about Tom and Mara before it ran out.

Emma apologised again for a less than pleasant welcome home. She told me that a few months after Tom and I had gone, she started having financial problems. She could not afford to pay the monthly mortgage instalments and other bills on her student-nurse's pay.

She asked her friend Beatrice to come and share the house and split the bills. Bea moved in but within a few months she lost her job and couldn't pay her contribution to the bills. Emma didn't feel she could kick her friend out and find someone else who could pay. Bea mooted the idea of starting a shebeen but Emma had refused to consider it. Emma started stealing medicines from the hospital and selling them in Southville. That didn't last very long. She was caught and expelled from her nursing course. She could have ended up in prison. Things were now worse than before. So when Bea suggested the idea of the shebeen again, Emma saw no alternative. After a couple of years, Bea got married and went to live with her husband. Emma continued on her own.

"I hope I haven't lost you too many customers tonight."

"On the contrary. I am glad it's all over."

"Over? You are not going to close it on my account, are you?"

"The war is over. I am going to look for a job. You need a long rest. Eventually, you will get a job. After all you have been through, they ought to make you a minister in the government. You are more educated than a lot of them. I am sure Tom will come home sooner or later. Together we shall manage like we did before the war."

"Well, I think you should continue with the shebeen until you find a job. I am not going to be doing much until I find out about Tom and Mara. It may take a short time but it may also take a long time. You seem to think I have some moral objections to the shebeen. I don't. If it's making money, you must continue it."

"I have to think about it, Tsiga. I have to think about it again."

I was worried and very tired. Emma prepared my bed in my old bedroom. I left her tidying up and went to bed. I think I had just fallen asleep when I suddenly woke up to find Emma, naked, next to me in the bed, her hand on my penis. I was shocked and enraged she could do that. I was shocked because I never thought that she could be unfaithful to Mara or so disloyal to me. I was enraged because she had taken it for granted that I would go along with it. Emma is not pretty but by anybody's standards she is attractive and Tom had fallen for her. But her over-confident attitude was misplaced.

After discovering her in my bed, the decision to quit 434 Sunningdale Road came instinctively. I was so furious and indignant I didn't utter a word. I jumped out of bed and got dressed. While I was throwing some clothes and a few other personal items into my bag, she tried to apologise. But I didn't want to hear. I didn't want to know. I simply shut her out and that was

3. Emma

it. I stormed out without so much as a glance at poor Emma. It was after slamming the door behind me that I told myself that I never wanted to see her again. It was only later, much later, that I admitted to myself that I had overreacted, but I never entertained any serious thought of going back. Although life had been more comfortable with Emma than I was finding it in the streets, I was independent and I felt happier.

Outside, I found no respite. The late morning air was hot and dry. The polluted heat made me feel slightly dizzy. I was surprised by the number of people on the street. The singing, cheering, hugging and dancing on the streets was euphoric. I felt edgy and irritated. Why were they all so happy? What were they going to get out of the independence celebrations?

That was three years ago. This time as I set off again for Emma's, I was fairly calm even though I was worried I might be attacked again on the way. I was also concerned about the reception Emma was going to give me. Of course, I knew she wasn't going to spit at me or slam the door in my face. I was bothered because I knew she would put on a little sentimental drama during which many tears would fall. I decided I wasn't going to mention anything about being mugged nor was I going to let her know that the sole purpose of my visit was to pick up the Colt. My story was going to be that I had come to collect a few of my clothes. As a matter of fact, I thought it a good idea to get as many of my personal belongings as I could comfortably roam with around Southville. Even with that story, there was no way she was going to let me walk in and walk out.

Emma has talent in the use of her emotions. I was going to have to play it by ear. The little expedition was going to take me longer than I wished.

When I arrived in Sunningdale Road, I got a little confused and thought I was lost. However, after double-checking, I realised I was at the correct address but number 434 had changed beyond recognition. Standing on the road, I could only see the roof of the house behind a new six-foot brick wall. Peering through an iron gate, I could see a bright red BMW on the paved and brightly lit driveway. The house itself looked bigger and was now white instead of the dull green it had always been. Initially, I thought that Emma had sold out to some well-to-do somebody and moved on. Wherever she was, I still needed my gun. If she had moved, there was a good chance the new owner might know where I could find her. I pushed the gate open and walked towards the front door. Perhaps, it occurred to me, she had won the national lottery. All of a sudden, I became apprehensive about my appearance and started feeling out of place. Because I could see no lights inside and it was very quiet all around the house, I felt like somebody up to no good. I heard no loud voices, drunken laughter or the non-stop music which were the hallmarks of Emma's evenings. The only time it had ever been quiet at 434 Sunningdale Road was between the small hours of the morning and about midday.

Convinced that Emma no longer lived there, I rang the doorbell and waited. I was uncomfortably debating whether to ring the doorbell again or leave, when

3. Emma

a light came on, the door opened and there stood Emma. After a brief moment, she flung herself at me and we embraced. She started sobbing. The whiff of a subtle scent rose to my nose. It told me the Emma of cheap strong perfumes had transformed. I felt a bit awkward and slightly embarrassed, not only because I knew I stank but also because I have never been good at dealing with emotional scenes. I couldn't think of any suitable word to say. I let her cry for a while before patting her on the back and telling her that everything was going to be all right. It was awful. Slowly, she eventually disengaged, took a step back and looked at me with a full smile and tearful eyes.

"We are not going to stand out here all night. Come in," she said, taking my hand and leading me into the house.

"At last, God has answered my prayers," she sighed, closing the door behind us.

She showed no sign of embarrassment at my physical state. Walking behind her, my dirty shoes sank deep into her rich carpet along the hallway. I could see that the house had been extended, redesigned and completely redecorated. Everything in the living room and, as I later found out, the rest of the house was new and looked expensive. Just about anything I set my eyes on was new. Still smiling through her tears, she invited me onto a white leather sofa. Dressed in rags as I was and carrying the mentality of a street survivor as I did, nothing could have been more absurd than me sinking into the comfort of that sofa. I felt like a character from some unlikely comedy. It was surreal. As I recall it, it was sheer torture. It was unbearable. I really did think of running out into the street screaming but I knew it wouldn't help much. To add to my discomfort, I was tongue-tied. I couldn't think of any appropriate word to say about anything. I didn't ask for it but Emma went to the kitchen and brought me a glass of water.

"You may find this hard to believe but earlier this afternoon I went to the shops to pick up a few odds and ends. I saw bottles of your favourite wine in the window and decided to buy a couple. One of them is in the fridge. Shall we open it?" she asked, standing in front of me.

"I don't remember ever having a favourite wine but, yes please, a glass of wine might work wonders for me," I said, struggling to appear comfortable. She went back to the kitchen and brought a bottle, a corkscrew and two crystal wine glasses on a silver-plated tray.

"God exists. He really does. Thank you for coming back, Tsiga," she said, clinking her glass to mine.

"You look good," I said, but what I really wanted to do was ask her how she had come into the money. She took my hands into hers and looked me in the eye. For that instant, she looked a sad old woman. But before she could say what she wanted to say, she broke down again. I felt raw. Her sorrow weighed on my mind like a fresh wound but I could think of no words to console her.

"You don't know how happy I am to see you again," she sobbed, smiling.

3. Emma

"Then try and not upset us both by crying," I pleaded, taking her hands into mine.

"Of course, you are right. I am just being silly. I should be thinking about how we are going to celebrate instead of working myself into a state like this. Let me go and just blow my nose and I will be all right," she said, standing up to go to her bedroom. My eyes followed her. She had lost some weight and looked more graceful in her simple outfit of white slacks, purple blouse and blue clogs. I sipped the wine and continued to wonder about where she had got the money.

"First things first, right?" she said, coming back into the living room.

"Right," I responded without an idea of what she meant

"I am hungry. You must be hungry too. I am going to start cooking. You are back in your own home. Do what you like. Take a look round the place and tell me what you think of the changes. Do whatever you wish and then join me in the kitchen. We are going to eat and drink but, God knows, we have a lot of talking to catch up on," she said pouring some more wine in my glass.

My tour of the house was perfunctory. I spent the time worrying about what complimentary remarks I was going to make. The trouble was I had nothing original to say about a pink bedroom or a marble-tiled bathroom. The only excitement I felt was when I saw the box in which I had hidden my Colt on top of the cupboard in my old bedroom. I didn't touch it. I rejoined

Emma in the kitchen and congratulated her on converting the old hovel into a fabulous little palace. I sat at the kitchen table where she was seasoning a duckling and began to feel famished again. After putting the duckling in the oven, Emma sat across from me and poured me another glass of wine. I asked her if there had been any mail for me. No, there had been none.

Putting on a serious air, Emma started by thanking me again for coming back. She coupled this with a heartfelt apology for coming into my bed, the event which had precipitated my unceremonious departure. She said dope and booze as well as her frail state of mind were to blame but she was not offering these reasons as an excuse. She had quit drugs for good and now only drank in moderation. She begged me to forgive her and I finally accepted her apology. But Emma hadn't quite finished. She wanted me to remember that without Tom and me, she would have never known a family life. Now that Tom was dead, I was the most important person in her life. I was her brother and she loved me. I listened to every word she said but I did not feel the same way as she did about our relationship.

Emma was an orphan. She was the daughter of a schoolgirl who abandoned the baby outside a convent within hours of her birth. Emma never discovered who her mother was. Her early life in the convent was hell – but she herself was no angel. The nuns who brought her up despaired. The tough little devil learned nothing and always got her own way. One night, when she was about nine, she walked out of the gates and never

3. Emma

returned. She took up life on the street, surviving by thieving and selling her body. Every day, whichever way she went, trouble followed her. She had numerous brushes with the law. Prison became a second home. She could never remember who or where, but when she was in her early teens somebody told her she was clever. Encouraged by this, she eventually got a job as a charwoman at Southville Hospital. She told Tom that the day she got the job she felt like she had risen from the grave. Inspired by other young women she saw at work every day, Emma decided she wanted to be a nurse but, of course, she did not have the qualification to start the training right away. She enrolled in a night school and worked very hard, day and night.

In the year before she started training as a nurse, Emma and Tom met at the night school. He was there teaching to earn some money to pay for his course in photo journalism. One thing led to another and, after a couple of years, they started living together. For once in her life Emma was happy – until the war came and swept my brother to his doom.

The smell from the oven was killing me and I told Emma so. She announced the food was ready. While she was serving the duckling, sauté potatoes and some fried wild mushrooms, she asked about Mara. I had nothing new to tell her except to reaffirm my belief that Mara was alive and that one day I would find her. Emma and Mara met once or twice but they hardly knew each other. All Emma knew was that I cared very deeply about Mara. Emma also wanted to know how I had been doing since I last saw her. I didn't really want her to know how tough my life on the street had been. Devouring her sumptuous food, I waffled and told her plain lies where I found it necessary.

After our lavish meal, Emma opened another bottle of wine and invited me back to the living room. Now, feeling less inhibited, I asked her if I could listen to one of my old John Coltrane albums on her new sound system. Emma wanted me to promise that I would not leave number 434 again but I could make no such promise. She insisted I promise that I would never leave without discussing it with her. Grudgingly, I made the undertaking. She then informed me that she had a serious proposal to make about both her and my future.

"Don't worry. I am not going to ask you to marry me or anything like that," she reassured me with a short little laugh, "But before we get to that, I want you to know how much money I've got and where I got it from."

It all began some four or so months after I had originally walked out of 434 Sunningdale Road. For Emma and Bea, business was just all right but not roaring. The two women had known each other for years. Hard times had always brought them closer. They had grown so close that quite often they would bed one man at the same time and then joke about it as they split the proceeds. Personally, I never cared for Bea. She was conceited, vulgar and mean. Anyway, one of Bea's regular punters invited them out of town to a weekend party. There were going to be eight couples and lots of food, drink and stuff to smoke. At first, Emma was

3. Emma

not keen to go but the punter offered a good sum of money in advance and reassured her and Bea there would be more if they were to remain discreet about the host and his guests. Emma agreed to go. On the Friday, the two girls were picked up by a chauffeur-driven white Mercedes Benz. On the way the driver said nothing and Emma and Bea tried to speculate about who their wealthy host might be. They had no idea who else would be there.

When Jerry came out of the house to meet them and before he could introduce himself, Emma recognised him. Not a week went by without Jerry's picture appearing on the front page of the newspaper. Emma's first impression was that he was a little older than the pictures in the paper but she found him more attractive in the flesh. Jerry was a household name. Even prostitutes like Emma and Bea knew he was the eminent barrister who was now the Attorney General. They also knew that as the businessman who owned a chain of supermarkets, pharmacies, bars, nightclubs, and many other ventures, he was reputed to be one of the richest people in the country. When Jerry finally spoke, Emma was overwhelmed by the calmness of his soft voice and the presence the man exuded. For a time after he spoke, she couldn't utter a word. The grandeur of the country house, the uniformed servants and his polite and attentive manner mesmerised her. She told me that the day she met Jerry she knew her life would never be the same again. Power, wealth, money, fame, they all sailed in her large brown eyes as her mind shuddered at the image of Tom, smiling and betrayed. Tom.

After being introduced to the other guests, who included two men whom she later discovered were the Minister of Justice and a High Court judge, Jerry took Emma aside. She couldn't believe her ears when he invited her to be the hostess of the party. When she said she wouldn't know how to do it, he told her that her main task was going to be staying by his side. All the servants would report to her. All she had to do was make sure the guests had everything they wanted and were happy. If she had any problems, he was there to help her solve them. He told her that he thought they were going to make a very good team. She understood what he meant.

With music Emma had never heard before playing in the background, Jerry ordered two of the servants to serve aperitifs on the patio. For three hours, Jerry, with Emma by his side, chatted with everybody and it was Emma who had to invite them all in to dinner. Jerry had briefed her on who was going to sit where. Jerry announced that everything on the table had been grown on his farm. The dinner lasted for ever. Everybody seemed to be having a great time. For the last course, Jerry, after dismissing the servants, personally offered cocaine, grass and dope. Everybody had a bit of everything. Then the music started grooving. Bea embarrassed Emma by starting to play the fool and inviting Jerry to bed but Jerry went dancing ever so close with Emma. Bea then lost all control. She passed out and had to be carried upstairs to bed.

Emma had no idea whether it was because she was drunk, stoned or in love but she started crying. The

3. Emma

next thing she could remember was finding herself naked, alone with Jerry in the pool. She could not recall when or how she got to bed. Jerry was there, giving her hot and passionate kisses. She really socked it to him until he exploded into joyous fragments of involuntary laughter. Her memory did not return until late the following morning when she woke up to find Jerry's experienced fingers working on her nipples. I asked her to spare me the personal intimacies. It was only then that she seemed to realise that she had been re-living her memories more than telling me of the beginnings of her affair with Jerry.

"I know you don't want to hear all this but I enjoy knowing I am responsible for it. It's the only time I have come close to understanding men," she said, looking directly into my eye. I looked into my glass of wine and thought of Tom.

When the rest of Jerry's guests were returning to the city after this dream weekend, he asked Emma to stay behind. They made love once more. Jerry said he wanted to know everything about her. She said because she felt completely at ease with him, she told him the true story of her life. She told him everything including the fact that she had to work as a prostitute in order to make ends meet. She said she found him very understanding and sympathetic.

Jerry came from a large hard-working city family. His father started off as a market stallholder, selling fruit and vegetables. With his savings and a loan from the bank, he bought a truck and got into the fruit and vegetable wholesale business. Through hard work, endurance and shrewd planning the business grew. By the time the old man died, the family had built a chain of supermarkets nation-wide but Jerry's father was better known for being an ardent nationalist than for his riches. He gave much to the Liberation Front, especially in the pre-war days. In all his nine children, he instilled hard work and ambition. At the university, where he excelled in law, Jerry had been the president of the students' union for two of the three years he was there. He graduated with first class honours, worked in a prestigious firm for two years before he set up his own company.

As he told Emma at the time, he had been married twice. With Selina, his first wife, he had two boys, Max and Joey, who were now at college in the United States. According to him, Selina had poisoned herself when the children were still quite young. When he met Maggie, he decided to marry her "for the sake of the boys." When she got pregnant, Maggie didn't want Max and Joey in the house. So he sent them to the USA. There was no longer any love between Jerry and Maggie but as a public figure he could not divorce her without running the risk of ruining his reputation. He was still living with her only for the sake of appearances. Finally he told Emma that if she stopped seeing other men all her financial difficulties would disappear. For Emma, this sounded too good to be true and she had nothing to lose by taking the suggestion seriously. She liked Jerry. When they made love, he didn't jump about like a schoolboy desperate for brutal pleasure. He made love slowly and sensitively. Before they drove

3. Emma

back to the city, Jerry took Emma on a tour of the farm. To show her how huge it was, he took her to the highest hill and pointed out various landmarks in the distant horizon that bounded the farm. A river and numerous streams ran through the farm. Emma thought it was more like a small country than a farm. There was even a natural lake where Jerry enjoyed fishing. From the top of the hill, she could see herds of cattle, flocks of sheep, pigsties and chicken pens. Apart from the lush green fields of maize, wheat and tobacco, the farm also had a wild nature reserve.

Back in the city, Emma was pleasantly surprised that Jerry wanted to continue seeing her. They saw each other as regularly as his legal, business and marital commitments allowed. Naturally, they had to be discreet. Apart from being a married man, Jerry nursed further political ambitions, even of one day having a go at the presidency. He did not want to have too many skeletons in the cupboard. He told Emma that his envious opponents were always on the lookout for any ugly rumours about his private life. He warned her not to be alarmed if she heard some outrageous stories about him. So to keep their relationship as secret as possible, they hardly saw each anywhere other than at 434 Sunningdale Road or at Capital Farm. Their relationship developed. Emma thought she had fallen in love with him but she knew that he did not feel all that seriously about her. But he liked her enough. When he started showing it, it was on a grand scale. It was to celebrate her twenty-fifth birthday that he decided to pay off the rest of the mortgage on the house, and to have the house rebuilt and refurbished. It was not all for her sake, he told her. He also wanted to be comfortable when he was with her. He couldn't stand not having what he wanted when he wanted it. Over time, he also gave her the BMW, a lot of other expensive presents and a sizeable cheque to live on every three months. Emma saw no reason to continue her "entertaining." So the wild nights at 434 Sunningdale Road came to an end.

Some six months or so into the relationship, Jerry changed. He started finding excuses for not being able to see her. He forgot to phone her when he had promised to. Reading the signs, Emma had suspected that it was all too good to last and prepared herself for what was about to happen. The thing that bothered her was that at the same time Jerry was easing himself out of her life, Bea also started distancing herself from her. One evening, Bea's ex-boyfriend dropped by Emma's house and told her that Jerry and Bea had been secretly sleeping together for some time. Emma couldn't believe the story but when she went to try and talk to Bea about it, her best friend refused even to open the door. Betrayed and humiliated, Emma resolved to forget both Jerry and Bea and go on with her life. Just before he stopped all contact with Emma, Jerry had paid a large sum of money into Emma's bank account. She didn't know whether the money was a pay-off for the humiliation or a payment for her silence or indeed for something else.

Emma was living quite comfortably. She had got over Jerry and she never wanted to see Bea again. She told me that one of the reasons she had hoped I would come back was that she wanted me to help her with suggestions on how to invest the money she had from Jerry. Her idea was that "we" should buy an off-licence or a small vegetable farm but she was open to any other ideas. I told her I knew nothing about business of any kind. If she wanted some suggestions from me, she would have to give me more time.

"Of course, take your time. We are not in any big hurry. I want you to feel free and relax. You are in your own home. By the way, your room has changed a bit but I am sure you will find everything more or less the way you left it. Tomorrow or the day after, we should go shopping and get you a few clothes and anything else you need."

After the meal, she wanted to show me round the house but I wasn't really interested. Instead of telling her the truth, I told her I was feeling lazy because I was full of food and the wine was getting to my head. We moved from the kitchen to the living room. She asked me how I wanted to spend the rest of the evening. I told her I wanted to try and dig out some clean clothes, have a bath and go to bed. She went to fetch another bottle of wine only to discover there was none left. I didn't think we needed more wine and asked her not to bother going out for some.

"All right, you stay here but I am going to pop out quickly because I feel we should celebrate tonight. I won't be long. None of your disappearing acts while I am out," she said, laughing. I told her not to worry. She left. I sat sipping my wine until I heard the car reverse out of the driveway and purr away.

The only way I was going to be able to leave was by escaping. My suspicion was that, for a day or two, Emma would keep me under lock and key. A day or two I didn't mind too much. I wanted to cut my hair, shave off my beard and have a long soak in the bath. I tried to remember some of the clothes I could wear after the bath. I promised myself that I would throw away my old bag and get a new one. There was also Emma's cooking and a long night's sleep to look forward to. No, this wasn't going to be bad. Alone, of course, the first thing I wanted to do was find my pistol. But something else was on my mind. I was no longer sure that I just wanted to get my gun and go. I had no food, shelter or a job and here was Emma giving me the best food, a comfortable home and a good prospect of earning my own living. It wasn't as though she had tried to murder me by coming into my bed. Living in the street was hard. I decided it was foolish to run out of Emma's house into the street. If she gave reason again, I could always leave after that. I made up my mind to consider everything and make a final decision in the bath but for that night, I was going to stay. I went to what had been my room. It was completely transformed. There was a new cupboard, a new carpet, a new bed and new curtains.

The cardboard box in which I had hidden the Colt was sitting on top on the cupboard. I took it down and placed it on the bed and started rummaging through a lot of papers, documents and letters and other things

3. Emma

under which I had concealed the gun. I knew exactly what I was looking for and in no time I found it. There it was still in the old newspaper that I had wrapped it in three years before. To my surprise it was in a very good state. It was still reasonably well oiled and fully loaded. It was like a reunion of two old friends. I thought of the times and places I had been in with that gun during the liberation struggle. I was so pleased I felt like a little boy with a new toy.

Mara's small and neat handwriting on one of the envelopes in the box caught my attention. I took out the letter and re-read it. For old times' sake, I wanted to read all her letters again – so I started looking for the rest. Going through the letters, I discovered Emma had mixed Tom's letters and mine together in the cardboard box. Although it was not important, I wondered why she had done that. As I went along, I separated Tom's letters from mine. Since his letters were now mine, I told myself that, one day, I should take time and go through them. I was looking through a pile of envelopes mostly addressed to Tom when I came across more of Mara's handwriting on an unopened envelope. I ripped it open and was surprised to find it was from Mara to me. I sat on the bed and read the letter. I read all the four pages quickly but I wasn't taking in the meaning of the words I was reading. Before I got to the end of the letter, my hand was shaking uncontrollably and my heart was palpitating fast and hard. Tears were rolling down my face. I felt a sharp stabbing pain inside my head. I was hot and began to sweat. I was frightened. I thought I was dying or going mad when my whole body started shaking like some reed in a fast river. I collapsed on the floor and wept. I have no idea of how long all this went on but, when it stopped, I was so angry with Emma that I told myself I hated her. The letter had been sitting in that cardboard box for over five years and yet when I came back from the battlefields, she had said she was sure there had been no mail for me. God knows how many times I asked her. My mind was in turmoil. I knew that if I waited until Emma came back, there was a danger I was going to lose my self-control.

I decided to leave. Without a second thought, I took the pistol and Mara's letter into the living room where I put them in the inside pocket of my coat. Purely by chance, I noticed a glass bowl full of coins on top of the sideboard. I took a handful and put them in my back pocket. I put my jacket on, picked up my old bag and walked out of the house. Back in the streets again, I wasn't sure what I wanted to do or where to go. I started walking towards the local shopping centre but I changed direction when it occurred to me that I might run into Emma. I turned round and started walking towards Baxter's Wood. I wanted to test fire the old Colt just a couple of times to make sure it was still working properly. Of course, I couldn't do that in the middle of Southville. No matter what, I promised myself, I would only use it to defend myself or, if really necessary, other people as well. Until then, I wasn't going to let anybody know that I had a gun.

After walking for a while, I changed my mind about going to Baxter's and decided to find somewhere I

3. Emma

could read Mara's letter again. Because it was already dark I had to read it either under a street lamp or near a shop-front light. That would be no good. I would read it in the light of day the following morning. In the end, I went to a late-night bar. I spent the rest of the night in a rusting car on the outskirts of the suburb.

On Tuesday morning, I woke up with a serious hangover but the first thing I did was to read slowly Mara's letter again. My first impulse was to jump up and go to see Jerry at his office in town but after reflecting I decided against it. The first time I had tried to see Jerry, I went to his office and his secretary told me that unless I wanted to see him about some legal or commercial business, my best bet was to try and see him at his house. When I tried to visit him at home, his guards sent me away at the gate. I didn't want to suffer the same humiliation again. I decided in my mind to try and see him at Capital Farm. It was very clear that if I had one hope in hell of finding or learning what might have happened to Mara, the only person who could help me was Jerry. This was Tuesday but, as Emma had mentioned several times, he went to his farm only at weekends. I would go and see him on Saturday.

I thought about Emma and felt that I might have been both unfair and harsh. She was wrong to have assumed that the initial 'T' on the envelope stood for Tom rather than me but it was not as though she had deliberately tried to hide the letter from me. Anybody could have made the same mistake. I still wished she had mentioned that there had been this letter even if it was for Tom. I would have known it was mine from Mara's handwriting.

I also felt slightly guilty that after she had talked so much about Jerry, I didn't let her know that I had also met and known him through Mara. I don't know why I didn't tell her but perhaps it was because it seemed irrelevant at the time. No, I did not feel exactly remorseful but, if I were going to see Emma again, it wouldn't be before my meeting with Jerry.

I had a suspicion that Emma, with nothing to do all day, would spend her time driving up and down the streets of Southville looking for me. I wanted to avoid running into her at least until after I had seen Jerry because I didn't really want to have to explain everything to her. It was for this reason that I left Southville for the city centre on Tuesday afternoon. Apart from the time I was at the university and during the struggle for freedom and democracy, I have always lived in Southville. Although I have no house I can call my own there, I still feel Southville is my home. I can't recall ever spending even one night in any part of the city outside Southville. If it had been in my nature to want to get to know people or get close to them, I would be friends with half the suburb. The suburb has a reputation of being a tough place. Even now, I feel proud that I know every corner of it – as well as how to survive in it.

Of course I had been to town on numerous occasions before but I was a little edgy when I got there on Tuesday afternoon. I couldn't remember ever having spent the night in the city centre. If I got into trouble

3. Emma

with the police for any reason, I was going to lose my pistol and stood a fair chance of going to prison for keeping it without a permit. If I were to be knocked down by a car and die in the street in my dirty underpants, I trusted that one or two people in Southville would come forward to identify who I was. In town, nobody would know or care.

On the way into the city, I remembered that Twoboy or somebody else had told me that if I was ever stuck in town and needed somewhere to spend the night, the waiting room at the main railway station was a good place. Generally it was noisy but nobody would give me any aggravation. I spent the first four nights in the railway station waiting room. Each night I shared the place with a mixed bunch of different people but there were also quite a few other homeless people who came every night. The waiting room was reasonably clean. The only things I didn't like were the smell of disinfectant and people talking late into the night.

Surviving in the city centre proved a little easier than in Southville. I mean there are a lot of rubbish bins in Southville but one rarely finds anything worthwhile. In the heart of the city, the bins, although fewer, are bigger and richer. The real bonus is that there are not as many dogs and cats to do battle with over a greasy bone. When someone throws you a coin, it is more likely to be a silver one. But I have to admit I miss the ambience of the township. In Southville, most ordinary people look you in the eye even though they talk down to you. You still feel like a human being. In the city, they glance at you from the corner of their guilt-ridden eye, throw you a coin or two and then hurry away from you like you were the plague itself. Those who don't want to give you anything or have nothing to give try to avoid eye contact as if you were a fly-infested wound. Reminds me of that dandy. He was in a dark business suit, briefcase and all. He looked happy but in a hurry. He threw me a coin but I couldn't catch it. As he hurried on, he looked back, perhaps to see if I was picking it up. Bang! His head hit a lamp-post and the self-satisfied smile on his face turned into a grimace of pain. His briefcase dropped to the ground. Initially, I really felt for him and was about to go and see if he hadn't cracked his skull but something came over me. I started sniggering and then I was gone.

On the Friday night, just as everybody was settling down, a group of railway policemen invaded the waiting room and threw out those of us who were not bona fide passengers. The eviction was taking place quite peacefully until one old man refused to move.

"Where do you expect us to go at this time of the night?" he asked in a weak, husky voice.

The frail and toothless old man must have been over eighty. The policeman who answered him couldn't have been more than twenty.

"I don't care where you go, Dada, just get out of here. This is not your home. As far as I am concerned, all beggars can disappear from the face of the earth."

The young officer's response angered a lot of people. A middle-aged man started telling the policeman some home truths. A second policeman hit the middle-aged man on the head with a truncheon. All hell broke

3. Emma

loose. I walked away. Of course, it was cowardice. But I also had a gun on me. I didn't want to be provoked into shooting a policeman or two. Nor was I ready yet to be arrested for the possession of an illegal weapon. I started heading towards City Park where I finally found a bench in a secluded area and I lay down. I was so uncomfortable it took me a long time to fall asleep. I dreamed I was travelling with General Tongo, who had been the commander of the liberation army during the struggle. In the dream, he was making jokes which kept me in tears of laughter. When I woke up, Fatnose was at my throat.

4. TWOBOY

Even now, I still can't understand what was going through Emma's mind when she sneaked into my bed that night. I cannot recall saying or doing anything to make her think I might want to sleep with her.

After that incident I was out on Sunningdale Road I was very anxious, almost desperate, to know what time it was because I didn't know where to go. If it was after five or just before five in the morning, I was going to go to a café I knew opened at five. If it was a lot earlier I was either going to wander about or go and hang out in a nightclub. But I had no way of finding out what time it was. I wasn't going to spend a fortune to shelter in a nightclub for a mere two or three hours. It wasn't cold nor was it raining. I decided to walk to the café anyway, taking the longest way to get there. I had plenty of time and a lot of problems, I reminded myself. I needed to be alone to sit down and think seriously about what I was going to do.

Under the dim street lights, I walked while Southville slept. I wondered if Emma was awake or sound asleep too. I hadn't felt so lonely in a long time.

Tsiga

Everything that came into my mind seemed bleak. The thought of going back to the house did occur to me but I found it too humiliating. I realised that turning my back on Emma meant I no longer had a place I could call home. I had friends. I could sleep here tonight and there tomorrow but for how long would I be able to do that? I had some cash but it wasn't much. How long I lived on it depended, of course, on how frugal I was. But I knew I couldn't possibly live on it for more than a couple of months at the most. Well, if things became really impossible, I reckoned, I could borrow from some of my well-off friends. But before borrowing, I had to know when or how I was going to repay whatever I borrowed. I had no idea of when or how I could do that. No, borrowing was a bad idea. I made up my mind that, in fact, it would be altogether better if I could avoid all of my friends until I had sorted out my basic problems. The best way for me was to face my problems by myself. I didn't want my friends feeling sorry for me or to live off their charity. If I couldn't take it, I could always eat humble pie and go back to Emma. The bottom line was that I was going to suffer but I was not going to die.

With my bag over my shoulder, I arrived at the café and found it was still closed. There were some plastic tables and chairs outside. I sat down and did some serious thinking about the future. The first important conclusion I reached was that I was definitely not going to go back to live with Emma. That was out. I was going to try and expunge her from my mind. It was a horrid

4. Twoboy

thing to do to her considering how kind and generous she had been but it was time I stood on my own feet.

As long as I could, I would continue searching for Mara but I also needed a job and a home. If I found her we would need both the money and somewhere to live. I was sure Mara would prefer not to have to depend on Emma as I had done for some time. I also realised that it was important to look for some work while I still had a little money. If I didn't get a job soon, I would end up in a dilemma: no home, no job; no job, no money; no money, no home.

My prospects for a decent job were no longer as bright as they had been after our victory. As a veteran, I could have applied for any high civil service post which I knew nothing about and got the job, but I had qualms about that sort of thing. If I was going to get a job, I wanted a job I knew I was qualified for and would enjoy. Anyway easy jobs for war veterans were no longer available. I had a degree in physics and an unfinished Masters. Realistically, the only job I could get was as a science teacher. I thought I would try and teach in a secondary school for a while. Although I hated teaching, it was the only job I was qualified for. I knew I had an attitude which was not popular with the government but there was no harm in trying anyway. Until I got a job, I had no idea of what I was going to do for food when the money ran out. I was going to have to eat whatever I managed to find and shelter where I could. There was plenty of space between the heavens and earth, I told myself.

Suddenly it occurred to me that someone I knew might come to the café or pass by and see me sitting there alone at that time of the day. I didn't want to have to explain anything to anybody. I picked up my bag and started walking up towards the hill. I don't remember thinking anything important as I walked round Southville until the sun came up. I was trying very hard not to feel too down about my situation but depression soon caught up with me.

I started thinking about Tom. I felt sad. He resurrected himself in my mind. No, I saw no ghost. It was him all right, with his easy-going smile. We had to talk. I needed to talk to him about my problems. He was a good listener. I told him how much I loved and missed him. He said I should not regret his death. Instead, I should remember that one day, I too would die but that didn't mean I shouldn't fight for life with everything I had. I assured him I did not blame Emma for my troubles. He said he knew that I didn't. We remembered conversations we had had, things we had done together, people and places we knew as well as humorous moments we had shared. Tom kept on telling me to have no regrets – saying it was a waste of time. I felt happy again.

When I stopped thinking about my brother, I realised it was late afternoon. My feet were aching. I could hardly stand on my legs. I was shaking from the heat and fatigue. My lips were parched. My stomach was growling from hunger but, most surprising of all, tears were rolling down my cheeks. Embarrassed, I wondered why and how long I had been crying. I pulled myself

4. Twoboy

together and worked out where I was. I found myself in the west of Southville, near where Pa used to live before Tom and I were born. I hadn't been to that part of Southville for years. I remembered the name of the street where Pa used to live but I couldn't remember the number. Anyway, I was too weary, too hungry and too thirsty to contemplate a short pilgrimage. I made my way to the local shops.

The local shopping centre was now bigger and busier than I remembered it. The evening rush hour had already begun and there was a lot of movement all over the place. I found a supermarket and bought a sandwich and a soft drink. I walked to the nearby bus shelter and sat down for my meal. I felt quite heroic for having been on my feet for so long. I was enjoying my rest and my mind was in oblivion when, suddenly, I actually heard Tom's voice. No, this was not my mind playing tricks on me; it was real.

"Thank you one, thank you all! Thank you. Change! Change! Please ladies and gentlemen! Change!" I heard him shout and my heart began playing havoc. It was my brother's voice. I abandoned my sandwich and drink to seek out the voice. Slowly, I made my way through the crowd. He wasn't far. The closer I got to him, the more he sounded just like Tom. I first saw him from the back. From the height, it could have been Tom. This man was thinner than Tom but then I hadn't seen my brother in over ten years.

"Could you please spare some change, madam? Thank you, thank you," he addressed a well-heeled woman who walked by without giving him so much as a glance.

He was dressed in a worn-out long black leather coat, a pair of dirty blue jeans, and soiled cowboy boots. That alone told me it wasn't Tom. Tom would never dress like that. I didn't know whether to feel relieved or disappointed. But then when I saw his face, my mind whirled into confusion. All my energy seemed to ooze out of my body. For a moment, I thought it was a hallucination. There was Pa, as a young man, right in front of my eyes. Not even the dreadlocks and beard could hide the fact that the man looked a better reproduction of Pa than Tom or me. The hairline, the eyes, the nose and the chin were Pa's. The small ears and the mouth were slightly different but not that much different. All that and Tom's voice led me to one conclusion: this fellow, whoever he was, had to be my father's son. There was no way it could all be reduced to coincidence. I don't know what came over me but I walked right up to him and looked him straight in the eye. I shall never forget the look of surprise that froze on his face the moment our eyes met. How I wish I could recall the thoughts or feelings I had in those few moments. With my hands trembling, I took out all the money I had in my pockets and in the bag and put it in the dirty blue basketball cap at his feet before hurrying away. I remember feeling like I had just performed some religious act for the atonement of my sins. All my troubles were gone. I felt serene, strong and free as I strode through the crowds. I felt a cool breeze blow through to my sweating armpits. A painful smile wrung

4. Twoboy

my face when I remembered that the man hadn't even thanked me for the money. I knew he was too shocked to think of doing that. I was so pleased to have escaped his gratitude.

"Hey, mister!" I heard him call out behind me – but I chose to ignore him. I walked faster and quickly disappeared into the crowd. If he caught up with me, I decided, I would deny ever having set eyes on him before, let alone giving him money.

I found myself on the way to Southville business centre. It was a relief to be away from the crowds. Along the road, once again, Tom's face imposed itself on my mind. He was smiling. He was telling me I had done the right thing. He reminded me never to regret anything. I told him I was no longer afraid of running out of money simply because I no longer had any. I didn't want to spend all my time worrying about money. I wasn't going to allow myself to be a prisoner of the damn stuff. If I was going to survive, I was going to survive on my brain and not on any money. I had no shortage of reasons or rationale to justify my generosity to a man I didn't even know.

I do not know whether it was several hours later that the ghost of my brother departed and I stopped tramping through Southville. Thirst, hunger, exhaustion and lack of sleep eventually forced me to sit down. I had no idea of where I was but it didn't matter. My mind was in a deep dark state. I wasn't sure whether I was dead or alive. My body ached. So did my soul and my spirit. Everything ached. I realised it was dawn but of which day I knew not. I tried to work out how long I had been on the streets but I found it confusing and gave up. If I couldn't work out the time, the least I could do was find out where I was. It then took one small glance to realise where I was. I laughed and it hurt. It was reassuring to discover I still had enough strength to laugh. I laughed because I was back at the same spot at the same storefront I had been earlier. No, I hadn't been there all the time, I was sure. The shopping centre was now deserted. Momentarily, I felt terribly lonely. Pathetic, feeling sorry for myself like that. I wondered how long I was going to survive. Just then, the environment encroached. First, I heard the distant sound of a bass guitar coming out of some nightclub. Then I felt a warm breeze slowly creep up, all over my face. Barely audible footsteps registered in my ears. My heart started pounding.

Like a butterfly, he came and perched beside me. I didn't bother to turn my head to look at him. Instinctively, I knew it was him. The fear I felt when I first heard his footsteps evaporated. The silence went on for ever but finally the man with Pa's face and Tom's voice spoke.

"Who are you doing all this for?" he asked. Now that he was not shouting or pleading for some change, his voice sounded even more like Tom's. I desperately wanted to look into his face to make sure it wasn't Tom but there was no point in that because I knew it wasn't. His question invited debate. I had no energy for that. I remained silent. Another endless moment ensued. Without a word, he offered me a cigarette. I don't smoke but I took one anyway, I don't know why.

4. Twoboy

He lit it for me and lit one for himself. For the first time since I last spoke to Emma, my jaws opened to ask him if he might be my father's son but in my own mind I couldn't even frame the question.

"You have been following me," I stated rather than asked. He took his time before reacting.

"I think we need to talk," he said, his voice trailing off with emotion. Talking was the last thing I wanted to do. It seemed to require so much energy. I knew what I wanted to tell him. I wanted to tell him that we could talk another time but, for that day, I wanted him to leave me alone but I couldn't even tell him that. I just sat there feeling numb. I couldn't put him out of my mind because he was right there next to me. I thought what a remarkable coincidence it would be if it turned out that he was actually my stepbrother. Meanwhile, I think he began finding the silence too dense.

"Are you hungry?" he asked me kindly but sounding a trifle patronising. I was not going to make an issue of it. He was offering help. Was I going to take it or not? I couldn't make up my mind.

"Let me be very honest with you. I was at home but I couldn't sleep. I decided to take a walk but I am not one of those people who enjoy walking for the sake of it. So I decided I would go out and look for somebody to play chess with. Do you play chess, man?"

For some crazy reason, I burst out laughing. It hurt a lot to laugh so much but I simply couldn't help it. He admitted it was an odd question to ask at that time of the day and in that place. I turned and looked at him. I told him I liked him because he reminded me so much of my brother.

"If you don't know how to play, I can teach you, man," he said.

"I can move the pieces," I told him.

"Let's go to my place and have a game. It's better than sitting here doing nothing," he suggested, offering me another cigarette. I declined. He stood and picked up my bag.

"Come on, man. Let's go," he said, strolling away. I stood up and followed him. We walked in silence. My foot was now excruciatingly painful but I was determined to keep pace with him. I had no idea where he was leading me to but we were heading down the hill. My new friend whose name I still didn't know realised I was in great pain.

"Listen, man. Get on my back. I am going to carry you," he offered.

It sounded so funny I had to laugh again.

"What's so funny about that? You are crazy, man," he said, falling into a hearty chuckle himself.

Then he added, "By the way, I am Twoboy. Not my real name but everybody calls me Twoboy."

We didn't shake hands. I didn't tell him my name. Side by side, we walked in silence most of the way. As we got to the south-western edge of Southville, I wondered if Twoboy was some sadist who was luring me to my death. Of course it was a silly idea. He seemed a kind person. Still, I told myself to be vigilant.

"I need to rest my leg a while."

"See that van over there, man?"

4. Twoboy

I could just make it out in the dark. It was no more than forty metres away.

"That's home sweet home, man."

The van. No it was no van at all. It was a shell of a long burnt-out small minibus sitting under a tree and surrounded by long grass. On the outside, the windows were covered by yellowing cardboard wrapped in plastic. For some mysterious reason, the door on the driver's side still worked. Not only did it work, Twoboy had devised a contraption so that it could be locked. In case of burglars, I mused, and felt like falling into another fit of laughter. We got in. He lit a candle. I did not sit down so much as collapse on the floor. My knees just gave in. I sat on the carpet of newspapers and sighed. In fact, the whole interior of the van was wallpapered with newspapers. A fire hazard, I thought. I took another look into his face while he lit another candle. His similarity to Pa was uncanny. I couldn't put it out of my mind. Was he really my stepbrother? But how could I be certain? I desperately wanted to ask him all kinds of questions to establish the truth, one way or the other, but my guts failed me. I was frightened and excited at the same time and the moment passed.

"So, this is home," he said with a tinge of sadness in his voice and a ray of sorrow across his face.

"I hope you have some food," I said, trying to be as cheerful as I could.

He turned and looked at me with gentle eyes and a sardonic smile. It was true, my manner had changed. Before he spoke again, the dark ray of sadness on his face dissolved.

"Sure, man. We are going to have a midnight feast. Right?"

"Great," I responded.

Something akin to pride glowed. Even if he is not my father's son, I thought, I love this guy.

"Let me see what's on the menu..."

He pottered around and found a few things. Our big dinner consisted of mouldy baked beans, a very delicious avocado and a stale piece of bread. From somewhere, Twoboy had found half a bottle of red wine. The wine tasted more like vinegar than the real thing but, despite that, we relished our meal. Famished as I was, it seemed nothing had ever tasted better. Out of sharing and enjoying this simple food, my friendship with Twoboy was born. The only trouble was there wasn't enough of it but we didn't care. We had become buddies. We talked.

"Here, my man," said Twoboy throwing me a dirty old grey blanket, "You are in a four star hotel. Relax. Make yourself comfortable. Pass out, go to sleep, if that's what you feel like doing. Drinking water is in that plastic container over there. The toilet is any discreet place you find outside. If you need a wash, you know where the council baths are. Any questions?"

"No. Thanks for everything."

"Yeah, there is one more thing. It was one hell of a move you made out there. I know exactly how much money you've got left – zilch. It so happens that I had more money than what you gave me. The way I figure it is that we are going to add all our money together.

4. Twoboy

You look after half and I take care of the other half, okay man?"

I was going to protest but he put his hand up and said, "Don't waste your breath. That's the way it's going to be. No conditions. Come and go as you please. Okay, man?"

I looked him in the eye and slowly nodded my head in agreement. We shook hands on it.

"I hope you don't mind too much but I am just trying to get to know you..."

Asking simple polite questions, Twoboy got me to tell him my life story. I told him all about Ma and Pa. He asked if I looked more like one of my parents than the other. I told him I couldn't say because Ma died when I was an infant. Hadn't I ever seen photographs of her, he wondered. I told him she had always refused to be photographed. He found that odd. He wanted to know if Tom and me, as twins, were significantly similar or different. I told Twoboy I thought the basic difference between my brother and me was that he had been an extrovert whereas I might be described as an introvert. We spent a long time talking about Mara. He wanted to know everything about her. Twoboy was a good listener. Side by side, like corpses in a crypt, we lay down. Just as I was dozing off, he lit up and inhaled deeply.

"Sleep tight, brother man," he said.

"Night."

"Kick the hell out of my butt if I snore."

Hardly able to keep my eyes open, I chuckled at the thought that he might keep me awake by his snoring and then I fell into a deep slumber.

Tsiga

I dreamt about Mara that night. She was swimming. I was just sitting there, watching her with a book in my hand. I was thinking that if angels existed they must look like her. Then she came and started teasing me. She told me that if I thought I was ever going to marry her, I would be deluding myself. She had just found a new ambition in life. She was going to achieve notoriety as the woman who seduced the Pope. That was a peculiar dream.

When I woke up it was almost midday. Twoboy was sitting outside the van smoking and coughing and playing a game of chess against himself. I sat on the ground, leaning against the van and watched him making his moves. I felt incredibly at ease. It was a very bright day. Not a cloud in the sky. I had this feeling I was in a new country. Apparently, Twoboy had been out and got us some doughnuts and mango juice for breakfast. He had already had his so I took mine alone. He also gave me three lumps of sugar and a tablet of vitamin C. He told me if I was going to survive in the streets, I had to look after my health. This was rule one of the many lessons in how to keep body and soul together on the street that Twoboy was to teach me. I watched him play out his game.

"How about a game?" I asked, before light-heartedly adding, "After all that's what I am really here for, isn't it?"

He looked at me and smiled.

"I like you. So I am going to be honest with you. I don't feel like a game, man. I feel like talking. I don't

4. Twoboy

care what we talk about just as long as we talk. It's been a long time since I really talked to anybody, man."

I took the opportunity and tried to discover a few things about Twoboy.

Twoboy was six months older than I was. He knew absolutely nothing about his father. When Twoboy was just over a year old, his mother met a man and they fell in love. She didn't want him to know she had a child with somebody else. She married the man and they moved away to Mutare, leaving Twoboy in the care of his devoted grandmother. He grew up believing that his grandmother was his mother. Once in a while, his mother would visit him but to him she remained a stranger. His granny died when he was sixteen. His mother came to the funeral and that was the last time he saw her. He knew she had four other children, three girls and a boy.

Twoboy was brought up in a rented two-room apartment in Southville. Whilst she lived, his grandmother, a humble woman, struggled to make ends meet. Her ambition was to see her grandson educated. All the little she had she passed on to Twoboy when she died. For about four years after the death of his grandmother, he managed to look after himself and continued going to school. But being a teenager with no experience of financial responsibility, he wasn't good with money. After selling everything he found himself with nothing and couldn't pay the rent. Naturally, although sympathetic, the landlord had to throw him out. He gave up school and started a life of drifting from one job to the next. Nothing seemed to be working out for his young and restless soul. Penniless, he ended up in the street but not before a spell in prison for drug dealing. At first, he found the homeless life hell; but now he could write all the rules of survival in the poor and sometimes dangerous streets of Southville. From what I could feel and understand, nothing at all seemed to bother him.

"Usually I eat only in the morning and in the evening but because you are here I thought we should have an extra meal. Just for today. Next time we do that again might be at Christmas. Even then, don't count on it, man," he told me.

"Don't worry about me," I said, "I am not a great eater. I can go a day or two without food."

"Yeah, man, but you can't do that on the street. You will be dead long before you know it. You've got to eat regular. Do you understand what I mean?"

I did and nodded. For this special lunch, Twoboy had bought a cucumber, a tin of corned-beef and a six-pack. The beer was rather warm but that didn't matter. We thoroughly enjoyed our treat. After lunch, as promised, Twoboy gave me my half of the money, which was a lot more than I had given him. He asked me to hide my money anywhere I thought it would be safe. He didn't want to know where I hid it. To show that I trusted him, I concealed the money under a thick layer of newspapers by the door inside the van. He warned me never to go round the streets with more than five dollars. With our small money business out of the way, Twoboy suggested we take a walk to the shopping centre. It was going to be a long day. For star-

4. Twoboy

ters, we hit the St. Peter's, a bar frequented mainly by low-lifers but it also had a kind of intellectual air about it. It also functioned as a social centre where a variety of groups regularly met to address social, political and other problems. As to why it was called the St Peter's, I never met anybody who could give me a satisfactory explanation. What was not in dispute, however, was that it was as old as Southville itself and was owned by a religious family who made a point of never setting foot inside its doors. I had been there a few times and I knew I didn't like it that much. It was always crowded, noisy and stank of tobacco, stale alcohol and disinfectant.

The moment we walked into the St. Peter's Bar, someone who knew Twoboy came up, embraced him and offered us a drink. I sat down at a corner table and watched Twoboy and his friend walk to the bar, hand in hand and in an animated conversation. Before they got to the counter, Twoboy was surrounded by several people who wanted to greet him or just exchange a few words. He knew everybody and everybody seemed to know him. There was that woman, midnight dangling from somewhere under the roof of her mind, blind drunk, utterly dolled out of this earthly life, demanding to know when Twoboy was going to take up her offer of free sex with her. She looked interesting. I got envious of him and forgot everything else. I wondered how long the young lady had to live. Next to her was this man, tall, thin, about forty, with a long holy face, eyes marinating in sorrow and seemingly desperate. He held onto Twoboy's hand. Later, I understood he had lost his wife and three children in a horrible bus accident. A street kid, just a kid, but old enough to be there, one dry tear frozen on his smooth black cheek, also waited to have an audience with Twoboy. There were those two men trying to pass glasses of beer to him. He accepted one and then found time to wink at me. I tried to reconcile the Twoboy I was looking at in this bar and the man I had met in the street begging for a few coins. Two different personalities. No wonder he was called Twoboy, I thought. A fat woman bought me a beer. I thanked her. I smiled at the man who bought the next one. One after another, people bought us drinks right through the afternoon. Twoboy and his friends invited me to join them at the bar but I preferred to sit alone.

By the time we left the bar, both Twoboy and I were zonked out of our minds. He amazed me by suggesting we go to another bar but I declined. We bought some fish and chips which we ate on the way to the van. When we got home, Twoboy wanted to have a game of chess but after arranging the pieces, he changed his mind. Instead, he wanted to know all about my experiences in the war. No sooner had I started telling Twoboy about my war stories than I realised he had fallen asleep, mouth agape and a smile on his roguish face. I gave him a pat before my own thoughts melted into a dreamless slumber.

When I woke up the next day and went outside, the sheer brilliance of the sunlight made me feel like somebody coming back from the dead. I had a bad hangover. Twoboy wasn't around. I felt lonely and acutely

4. Twoboy

melancholy. I hated my new life in the street. I told myself that if I was a reasonable and rational person, I should get off the streets, put my tail between my legs and get back to Emma. I thought about this for a long while and decided I wasn't going to go back to Emma. The truth was that I walked out on her not because she had come into my bed but because I hated myself for being so utterly dependent on her. It would be more humiliating to go back than to be destitute in the street. Whatever I had lost in home comforts by leaving Emma's house, I resolved, I would more than make up for in the real friendship developing between Twoboy and me. In fact, when Twoboy came back, all thoughts of going to Emma's evaporated. He happened to be in a very humorous mood and we laughed a lot.

After about a week of staying with Twoboy in the van, a pattern of how we spent our time began to emerge. Of course, each day was different but the general range of our activities was pretty limited. The first memorable thing about my relationship with Twoboy was that, despite all that talk about chess, not once did we ever have a game. A few times, we watched each other play alone but we never had a game against each other. We never discussed the pros or cons of playing against each other but it became an unspoken agreement that it was sort of taboo for us to play each other. I still think that was very odd.

Apart from the possibility that Twoboy may have been my half-brother, there were few things we didn't talk about. The only subject we talked little about was politics. The first time Twoboy and I discussed politics in any depth was when the government announced that it was going to "clean up" the capital. Squatters, beggars, prostitutes and other undesirables would no longer be tolerated on the streets of our nation. This was to help the ailing tourist industry. Squatters in derelict buildings and the poor who lived in shanty towns were not an attractive sight for the eye of the tourist. Beggars and criminals, who seemed to grow in numbers by the day, were a nuisance because they harassed respectable people. The tourist industry had suffered enough and something had to be done. Within days of the announcement, the police were in action. Thousands of people were rounded up and "deported" to rural holding camps where they were to be kept until the government had decided what to do with them. It was pure luck that we missed wave after wave of arrests. Before the plan took root, poetic justice came to the rescue. Walking home alone in the evening, the wife of a senior government minister was inadvertently arrested and sent to one of the new camps. Despite all her protestations, the police were convinced she was a prostitute. Whether this was true or not became a matter of conjecture on the part of the public. When the newspapers splashed out the story on their front pages and questions were asked, the government, terribly embarrassed, abandoned the whole operation. Twoboy was so incensed by such blatant corruption he was ready to throw himself into politics. It took me days to persuade him that politics was not a career for honest people like him.

4. Twoboy

Normally on Sundays, we would go for long walks to Baxter's Wood unless it was pouring with rain or sizzling hot. We picked mushrooms we knew we could never eat because we had nowhere to cook them but, more importantly, that was where we shared our endless daydreams. We also talked about the past and the present. In all of our discussions, Twoboy's biggest regret was that there was no God. Oh, yes, he genuinely regretted that, holy man that he was.

Usually we ate together but sometimes Twoboy stayed out late, enjoying a drink with friends. So on those occasions, I ate alone. The principle of our menu was that it had to be cheap and ready to eat. Inevitably, we survived on fish and chips, hamburgers and tinned food. It wasn't easy, especially since we had no idea of when this kind of life would come to an end. I certainly knew I was living one day at a time.

There was another bizarre happening in my relationship with Twoboy. Once or twice a week, we each went to the municipal baths for a wash but for some reason or other we never went on the same day in all the three years we knew each other. The first few times I visited the baths, I used to invite Twoboy but he never accepted. When I stopped asking him, he seemed more comfortable. In my mind, I had no doubt that he had no better reason other than that he was afraid to discover that I had the same birthmark on the back of my shoulder as the one I knew he had in the same place. I know it would have been easy for me to be wrong about this because I was obsessed by the idea that Twoboy was my father's son. But I also know that wasn't all.

Over the course of those three years, we had quite a few exciting evenings and nights. It was interesting for me that some of these tended to come soon after one excursion or another in our joint efforts to try to locate Mara. I have to say no one else did more than Twoboy to help me find Mara. But now and again he would go out and come back with one or two young ladies. When he brought one girl home, he would always offer to let me get it on with her first. When he brought two, I was always a disappointment to the woman, to Twoboy and, frankly, to myself. For me, apart from my fidelity to Mara, I was seriously concerned about AIDS. But there was that one time I forgot Mara and took the risk. It was with this do-gooder who claimed she was doing some research on homeless people. She had these wonderful thighs and wore a Parisian perfume. I wish I could think of some convincing excuses but, well, I just couldn't resist her. It was very exciting. She was a great screamer – calling out the holy names of Jesus, Mary mother of God and the Lord himself. When it came to the ultimate satisfaction, it was her mother she invoked. I shall never forget her. She enjoyed our sexual adventure so much she thought we should try and have a relationship but I told her that, unfortunately, I was already spoken for. Yes, she did seem surprised that a man in my lowly position didn't want her. For days after that, Twoboy had pleasure mimicking her and suffering helpless giggles. On the cold floor of the van, she was the greatest fun I had had in years. After that I invariably respectfully declined any offer of sexual favours. I know Twoboy was seriously bothered

4. Twoboy

that I had snobbish moral values. He tried very hard to defeat me over this issue but I always ended up going for long walks to avoid it. At the end of the day, however, I won his highest accolades for loving and living for Mara. The real miracle of my friendship with Twoboy was that we never fought. Not even verbally. I honestly do not think there was any deliberate effort to avoid arguments. We simply got on very well.

For us life continued as an acceptable monotony until one morning, some eight weeks or so ago, an elderly homeless man was found stiff, like a rat, in some alleyway. The police, and later the pathologist, found there was nothing suspicious about his death. Apparently he died of natural causes. He had no family and was homeless. The city council buried him in a communal grave and that should have been that. But in his great wisdom, the police commissioner called a press conference to announce that several thousand dollars had been found on the dead homeless man, stuffed in the various pockets of his tattered clothes and in the lining of his old coat. It was front page news in most papers, high and low. At the time, it didn't bother us much. We thought of it as just another unusual story but I could not understand why the police commissioner needed to make such an announcement. He wasn't even appealing to the late man's family to come forward and claim the money. But Twoboy immediately saw what the police chief was up to.

"Fucking hell! Do you realise what they're now trying to do?" Twoboy asked, sweat crystallising on his round forehead.

"What?" I asked, totally sceptical of whatever explanation he was going to offer.

"They are trying to get the unemployed hoodlums to clean the homeless man off the street. The police commissioner is inciting murder! I can't believe this, man."

I did accept that there might be some sinister motive behind the commissioner's announcement but I found it far-fetched to accept that he was inciting violence against the homeless. Twoboy warned me to mark his words. Before anybody knew it, gangs of unemployed youths in Southville started hunting the homeless. As the story of the old man had proved, tramps were not necessarily poor, the street thugs reasoned. Instead of waiting for the homeless to die in the streets, the gangs decided they would help to hasten them to their graves. The killings started. Within a week of the story breaking, three homeless men were murdered in Southville. Another nine, two women and seven men ended up in hospital with serious injuries. Although the gangs were not making any money, the violence against those who lived on the street continued and spread to other parts of the city. Despite belated efforts by the Minister of Home Affairs and the police commissioner at another media conference to undo their wicked mistake, life for homeless people got worse.

When the killings started, Twoboy and I, like most homeless people, had to change our ways. We lost our self-confidence because of what was happening on the streets that we thought we knew so well and where we had grown up. We now mostly went out only during

4. Twoboy

the day. If we stayed out after dark, we took all kinds of precautions on the way home. We stuck together more than before. At the van, we armed ourselves with a variety of small crude weapons like stones, sticks and bottles. It was bad. We were living in fear. We took turns to stay up at night just in case.

The gangsters began to get frustrated. They were working very hard and became more daring by robbing people on crowded streets in broad daylight but had little to show for it. Instead of leaving the poor people of the street alone, they devised a new code. To flush out those who were thwarting their efforts, the less money you had, the more violence you faced. It was madness. Week upon week, the number of murdered homeless people mounted. The amazing thing was that nobody was responsible – nobody got arrested. Public concern mounted. Finally, a couple of boys were arrested. Their trial took a long time to come to court. There was horror and disgust when the two young men were released without being charged because of insufficient evidence. The turmoil was not only among the homeless; it was national. Apart from issuing appeals for peace on the street, the Ministry of Home Affairs and the police did nothing to stop the murders. A few more people were arrested but nobody was jailed. Homeless people continued to die. One day, Twoboy and I started a serious discussion about the situation.

"What do you think the ruling class in this country is really up to, man?" Twoboy asked me, "Why don't they want to bring all these killings to a stop?"

"I don't know, but sure they don't like destitute people. So why should we expect them to do anything for us?"

"Yeah, man, you are damn right. It's foolish of us to expect anything of the selfish bastards. You know what I think, man? I think the only way out of this is to get organised and protect ourselves."

Typically, by the next day, Twoboy was out organising. He went all over Southville, talking to the many people he knew and meeting new ones. He talked even to those who had jobs and homes and solicited their moral support. Basically, he was simply encouraging homeless people to band together so that they could defend themselves more effectively. A simple objective. Twoboy didn't bother to ask me to help with setting up these groups; he knew I wasn't cut out that way. I was very impressed by his enthusiasm and dedication. He saw the establishment of these groups as the first stage on the long road to the political revolution that he believed our country so badly needed. But he had no illusions about how long that road was.

Tuesday arrived with clear blue skies and brilliant sunshine but for some reason I woke up with a thick lump in my throat. Before he went out to his new meetings for the homeless, Twoboy wondered if I was sick or something. I told him I was all right and not to worry about me. As the day wore on, I felt more and more depressed. The weather turned humid and black rain-clouds began to gather. By the time the inevitable thundery storm finally broke that afternoon, I was a nervous wreck. Hard as I tried, I found no explanation

4. Twoboy

for my state except this strong sense of foreboding. I knew the feeling because I had experienced it a couple of times before. I spent most of the day alone in the van, trying to work out what was wrong with me. Eventually, the storm exhausted itself. I got out of the van and sat outside. The cloudless sky returned. My mood began to lift. I watched the blue sky slowly turn to a glorious orange-red as the sun floated down below the horizon. I felt my usual self again.

I realised I was famished and wished Twoboy would come home soon so we could eat together. I convinced myself he was out drinking with some of his mates. However, when he came home soon after dark, he was stone-cold sober. For reasons best known to himself he had spent a fortune on a small mountain of sausage and French bread which for us was an enormous luxury. He also came armed with two bottles of cheap wine. I had never seen Twoboy in a stranger mood. He looked quite happy but I could also feel some internal rage going on inside him. He had never spoken to me so slowly or so deliberately. He told me the political situation in the country had to change. He was going to play his full part to bring about that change. His life was not going to be worth anything unless he was committed to something. I recall his every word. We ate and drank. The more we drank and talked the more I got worried. One moment I was talking to the Twoboy I had grown to know and the next moment, I was listening to a complete stranger. After our first bottles of wine we found our usual comfortable level. He told me he had been feeling like a caged animal all day. I told him it had been more or less the same for me. We put it all down to the humid weather.

To me, the question came and was delivered like a thunderbolt.

"In the sanctum of your mind, do you really believe that Mara is still alive?" He took a long pull on his cigarette. He looked at his cigarette in a very sensual way before he glanced at me. If it had been someone else asking me that question, I would have flown into a rage but instead I looked at the floor and said nothing. I remembered that the first time I felt the way I had been feeling all day was the day before Pa died and the second time was the day Tom actually got killed.

"You know I didn't mean it in any malicious way," he said apologetically rubbing his forehead,

"I was just wondering how long you are going to live for this woman. I think it's time we both went out there to be with the people. Wherever she is, Mara would be proud to see you fighting for the people, I know you can punch a hole or two in the establishment. Hell, man, you have got qualifications. You have got the brain. You know how they think. People need you."

I wanted to cry because I felt sorry for Twoboy. I had never felt sorry for him before.

"Hell, Twoboy. Why don't you do it? You have got twice the brains I have. Aren't you the world chess champion nobody knows about?"

"I am doing my bit. I have started doing my bit but I wanted us to be in it together. Is that asking for too much? Is that such a bad thing?"

4. Twoboy

"No it isn't. But listen. I spent years of my life doing my bit and we won the war. I know a lot of people who died or had their lives wrecked doing their bit. Isn't that enough? I don't want to die before I live. I am not your political revolutionary who is prepared to spend his life fighting for one lost cause after another."

"I don't know. Maybe you're right. You know, man, the reason I asked you about Mara is because I have this tight feeling that you are going to find her real soon. I hope you didn't misunderstand me. And you know something else? I would give my life to be there when you two meet again," he said, a painful grin wringing his sad face.

I got the feeling that we were dancing around an issue. We were avoiding the subject. I looked at Twoboy and told him, "Twoboy, you know I love you. And I know you know what I mean."

"Yes, I know. Same flesh and blood. The moment I saw you, I knew you were my brother. You want to know how I knew? – I felt it."

"I have been meaning to talk to you about this from day one but for some reason I kept on putting it off," I told him, unsure of how to proceed.

Twoboy looked at me with a smile, tears welling in his eyes.

"Same here. Since the day we met, I have also been meaning to ask you about it. I didn't ask because I thought I would be very disappointed if it turned out that you had some doubts about it. For me it was like a beautiful dream and I didn't want to kill it. Can you understand what I am saying? Oh, man!" he said, hugging me.

We both cried on each other's shoulder. It was painful.

"I think we should drink a toast to the old man," Twoboy suggested.

He refilled our glasses and we drank to Pa, Twoboy's mum and to Ma.

"I still can't understand why we haven't been talking about all this before," I said, more to myself than to Twoboy.

"Don't worry about it. It's not the sort of thing that happens every day."

"You know what we are going to do?" I asked him.

"I have already thought about it. Mum has suffered a lot. I think it would be better if we left her to enjoy whatever little happiness she may have now. Anyway, I think we should at least wait until we have found Mara and seek her advice."

"I know you and Mara will adore each other."

"I have a problem. I can't understand why I am feeling hot one moment and very cold the next," he said in a pensive voice.

"It's your politics that makes you feel that way," I joked, "You will be all right in the morning. Let's try and get some rest now."

We finished the last bottle. I stood up, stretched and did a few body movements. Twoboy stood up and gave me a big hug. There was fear in his eyes. He looked hopelessly distressed. I didn't know how to help. I persuaded him to try and get some sleep.

4. Twoboy

"Shit, man, I have run out of cigarettes," he complained.

"Oh, don't you worry. You will get some in the morning," I said, trying to console him.

"Yeah, but you don't know what it's like to go to sleep without that last cigarette."

I had nothing to say to that. In his usual enchanting way, he started telling me this old story of a long affair he once had with a married woman. He rambled on and on until I could no longer hold off the sleep.

"Night, night now," I said.

"Easy on the dreams, main man. Like time, they can sometimes run out on you."

We both fell asleep.

Wednesday morning, just a week ago, I remotely recall him getting up and getting dressed. I wasn't ready to wake up or, to put it in another way, my eyes had no will to open, my consciousness refused to surface. My physical state had a lot more to do with the cheap wine of the night before than anything else. I vaguely remember him asking me for twenty-five or thirty-five cents because he didn't want to change a big note just to pay for a packet of cigarettes. I must have mumbled for him to check in my trouser pockets or something to that effect. I heard him close the door to the van. It was such agony to keep awake that I was praying he wouldn't try to wake me up when he came back. Without any effort, I drifted back to sleep. I still wasn't all right when I woke up around noon. I assumed Twoboy was outside playing chess against himself as usual. After a while, I called out his name but got no answer. I thought he might have gone out and wondered how he could be already drinking while I was still trying to recover from the night before. But then I started worrying about him.

As time passed, I got increasingly anxious about him. I decided that if he was not back within an hour, I was going to have to start looking for him. The odd thing was that I had never been apprehensive about Twoboy in this way ever before. No, we were not married and he could choose to do what he wanted to do at any time – but the one thing I knew was that he had never given me cause to worry about him like that before. My nerves of the previous day returned. After the hour I had given myself, I added another. Still he did not show up. I jumped out of bed, got dressed and decided to start with the kiosk where we usually bought cigarettes and other small items. I made sure I had some cash and then left.

The moment she saw me, Mrs Gore, the adorable kindly lady who ran the kiosk, started weeping. Of course I immediately knew something was seriously wrong.

"They have killed your friend. They showed him no mercy, the vicious hounds," she cried in the manner of a liturgy and continued, "They slaughtered him like an animal. And what had he done to them? Nothing! Nothing at all."

My heart pulsated so violently I thought I was having a seizure. Mrs Gore rushed forward and helped me to sit down. She did all she could to soothe me. After she gave me a glass of water, I felt slightly better. She

4. Twoboy

called one of her young sons to come and man the kiosk while she took me to her nearby house. I felt no energy at all in my body and my mind was boggled by questions and images of Twoboy as I sat down on one of her sofas. I asked her to tell me what she knew.

Twoboy had arrived at the kiosk some time soon after nine. He asked for his usual packet of cigarettes and paid but he was three cents short and Mrs Gore told him not to worry about it. He promised to give her the three cents next time. He lit up and chatted to her for a few minutes before he left, heading for the van. As he walked away, she saw three kids whom she recognised because they had robbed her a couple of times before. She didn't think they had come to rob her this time because even they knew it was too early for her to have made much cash. It had occurred to her that they might try to mug Twoboy but she already knew he had nothing on him since he owed her three cents. When they were some distance away, the next thing she witnessed was the thugs talking to Twoboy. All of a sudden, they set upon him with knives. Twoboy fought them as valiantly as any man could. There was a moment she thought he could have got away if he had tried to but he seemed determined to fight to the end. They co-ordinated their attacks and kept on plunging their knives into his body as if there was nothing sacred about a human life.

For her, it was a nightmare she never imagined she would witness. She had seen a few men killed but none so brutally. The only thing she could do was scream and scream to alert other people. Of course the cowardly butchers covered in Twoboy's blood fled when they saw people race out of their homes to help him. But it was too late. He was losing too much blood and sinking fast. Twoboy lay in a pool of blood. He was bleeding from wounds to the face, the neck, the chest, the back, and his arms. While Mrs Gore was trying to stop the loss of blood, a woman driving by stopped and offered to rush him to the hospital. Some of the people who had gathered carried him into the car and two of her neighbours drove to the hospital with him. Mrs Gore thought he was already gone by the time they lifted him from the ground. Even if he was alive, she couldn't see how he was going to make it with all those wounds. What devastated Mrs Gore was that when she first got close to him, he wore a half smile over which blood trickled to the ground and after he was gone, it remained there. There was no pain on his face. And there was no fear in his eyes. She would always remember him like that. As the car sped off, Mrs Gore sang "Amazing Grace" for Twoboy.

The police finally arrived about an hour after the incident despite the fact that Mrs Gore's son had telephoned them before Twoboy was taken to hospital. They took a statement from her, which included the descriptions of the three youths. Once she mentioned that she knew the young murderers because they had robbed her twice, the police accused her of wanting to get even with the robbers and lost interest in her evidence.

I thanked Mrs Gore. Before I took my leave, the big round woman saw me to the door and repeatedly advised me to be vigilant on the street. Outside her

4. Twoboy

door, I found the world had turned upside down. I walked away but I had no clue in which direction I was headed. Until I was out of her sight, I was worried Mrs Gore was going to call me and tell me I was taking the wrong direction for the hospital. Fortunately, she did not. More by chance than anything else, I happened to have taken the right direction. At the bus stop, waiting to catch a bus to the hospital, there was a very distinct moment I suddenly started feeling a great calmness. It was like the wind gently filling an empty hole. Given that my best friend had just been murdered the calmness seemed very unnatural. I thought here was a feeling that was masking a turbulent emotion to come. This feeling was to stay with me for the next three days. My mind was extraordinarily lucid. I was not afraid of anything or anybody.

At the hospital, they kept me waiting. Asked if I was a relative, I told the woman in charge that I was Twoboy's brother. I said it just like that, naturally. Nobody was about to make me prove it. Twoboy's body was already in the mortuary. An elderly man led me there. I had never been in a mortuary before and hated it. It was Twoboy all right in that cold metal coffin. It was just his face I saw. He was asleep. He was peaceful. Despite the several scars, he still looked handsome. I can't remember exactly how I felt but I know that I didn't cry or experience any anguish. I stood over him, looking at his face for about two minutes and then the old man took my hand and led me out. Before I left the hospital they told me they would release the body to me on Friday afternoon. Instead of getting the bus, I decided to walk all the way back home, to the van. On the way, I thought a great deal about life and death. By the time I got to the shopping centre, I had come to no fundamental conclusions except that there was really no need to be so terrified of death. Ideally, it would be preferable to die as painlessly as possible. I wished I could choose but acknowledged that only a very few people had any choice about the timing.

From a bottle store at the business centre, I bought several cans of beer and went home. I thought it would feel strange being there alone, knowing that Twoboy was never coming back. But I just felt numb. I didn't feel hungry. I sat in the van sipping my beer, a thousand thoughts on my mind. It got dark. I lit no candle. I felt more comfortable without any light. Some time later, I was startled by some voices outside and then a knock at the door of the van. It was Mr and Mrs Gore. I lit some candles and let them in. I offered Mr Gore a can of beer which he accepted. She, an avid church-goer, didn't touch the stuff. I thanked her for the food she had brought me. When they asked me, I told them that I had enough money to buy the coffin and that I didn't know how much it was going to cost to hire a hearse. But I assured them that the sum of money I had and what Twoboy had left was more than enough to cover the funeral costs. They made two suggestions. First, they offered to pay the cost of hiring the hearse. The second one was to have Twoboy's body at their home overnight on Friday to enable Twoboy's friends and acquaintances to say farewell. We arranged to have Twoboy buried on Saturday afternoon and they left.

4. Twoboy

Until Friday afternoon when we went to collect Twoboy's body, I spent most of the time in the van. My wish was to be alone but people kept on dropping by to offer their condolences and find out when the funeral was going to be. Nobody told me that word about Twoboy's death had travelled fast around Southville and that people from all walks of life were very angry about the inaction of the police over the deaths of homeless people. Somebody might have mentioned it but I don't think it sank into my head. The trouble is I don't remember much at all about those two days. What I remember very vividly is our arrival with the body of Twoboy at Mr and Mrs Gore's house. As we got near the house, the hearse ran into a sea of people. There were all kinds of people out there. I felt love for them all. What surprised me was to see the rich among the poor. There were as many men as women. It was like one of those dreams in which I couldn't wait for time to pass. I was convinced that we had just happened to run into a demonstration against the government. I just wanted the dream to be over. But when I saw some of the people weeping and wailing, I realised they were mourners. My mind lurched from appreciating this essence of humanity to feeling personal apprehension because I hate crowds. So I shrank. Retreated. It was a relief to become a spectator of my own emotions again. Apart from the crying, some people were singing and dancing. Some faces were drunk or smoked out of their minds. How could I forget that small group of women in blue uniforms singing their own church hymn while most of the men were shouting and singing political slogans. The scene was, for me, a little more than frightening. There were literally thousands of people. It took the hearse twenty-five minutes to complete the last five hundred metres. After the body had been taken inside the house, I felt a desperate need to be alone.

It took some time but eventually I realised that things were not as disorganised as I had imagined. I was learning fast. In fact, everything was being carefully controlled, but by whom I didn't know. The coffin was opened to show just Twoboy's face. People filed in to view the body through the back door of the house and went out through the front. Money, mountains of notes and buckets of coins, was brought into the house and counted before going out to buy food and drinks for the multitudes. I wished Twoboy was there to see how much people loved him.

When I got out of the house the next morning, the whole area around Mr and Mrs Gore's neighbourhood resembled a refugee camp. There were few people left but there was still a long queue waiting to file past the body. At about two o'clock in the afternoon, Mr Gore declared the body viewing over and he invited me to spend a little time alone with Twoboy. I stood looking at his made-up face for what seemed a very long time. The one childish thought I remember having was that maybe if I looked at him long enough and wished him alive, I might just see him rise from the coffin and dumbfound the world.

It took a good two and a half hours to cover the four kilometre journey from Mr and Mrs Gore's house to the

4. Twoboy

cemetery. Southville had not seen such a massive funeral cortege in a long time. Emotion caught up with me and I cried as we drove to the cemetery but my mind was miles elsewhere. The bright sunshine had started to dull. High, free riding clouds of rain started to gather as we got closer to the cemetery. I didn't like it. For the first time since Twoboy died, my heart missed a beat.

Sitting in the hearse, I had no idea of what was happening on the edges and in the middle of the crowd. As far as I could make out there was nothing out there, except madness. I decided I didn't want my funeral to be like that. If it was possible, I would have liked it when I am dead to be able to bury myself in a nice quiet corner, somewhere between the foot of a mountain and the shore of a lake. I felt tinned in that hearse. I was boxed in by the crowds. I wished I were dead with Twoboy. As we entered the cemetery, the day became darker. Everybody knew a storm was bound to break soon.

Up till the last week, Twoboy and I had counted ourselves lucky. And what I find I can't forgive is that they didn't just kill him but they slowly tortured him and finally slit his throat all because he didn't have a dime for them to rob. They slaughtered him like an animal. To sustain all those stab wounds, he must have fought them like a tiger to the very end. It's all like a nightmare that never took place but I know it happened only a week ago.

Tsiga

5. TOM

That must be the Mudzi River. I hope it has some water. Even a pool will do. My mouth feels unclean. Needs a wash. I have been smoking too much. I can't say I am thirsty but my lips feel parched. I should wash my face as well. I wouldn't mind some pool where I can actually bathe. It's been some time.

I am not sure I want to go into a village and ask for some water. Trouble with villagers is that after you accept their hospitality, they want to know everything about your life. They start asking you for your name, your father's name, your mother's name, where you are coming from, where you are going and the rest of it. I am not sure I want to be bothered with all that. Unless I am really desperate, I think I am going to avoid asking for water or food from villagers. But I have to give it to the rural people: generally they are more human, more understanding than those soulless urban immigrants.

It really is getting hot now. That trouble down there in my stomach must be the beginning of hunger. But hunger is all right. It comes and goes. It's thirst I cannot bear. When it comes, it stays with you until you do

Tsiga

something about it. Like digging a small well on the riverbed.

For once, today I can say I am glad both father and Tom are dead. It would kill them to see me in this state. Father would worry about how I look. He hated beards and wild hair more than anything else. I ought to have asked why. Tom would have been worried about my mind.

As twins, I think what we lacked in identical looks, we far made up for in similarity of thought. We played hundreds of games of chess. Not once did I beat him. He never beat me. Always stalemate. At the time it didn't seem remarkable. Same brain in two different heads.

Mara used to say that she wished she had been born in the past. She saw us there, a few hundred years back, in a life without the paper god called money. Our bush home would be built with wood from nearby plains and forests. Water would be drawn from a nearby spring. I could see her bathing in a secluded pool while her clothes dried in the sun on the bank. We would keep chickens that would really taste like chicken, goats, sheep and cattle. She would spend most of her time tilling the land. Every kind of crop would grow in our fertile fields. We would clothe ourselves in leather, furs, natural cotton and bark cloth. We would hunt for meat and clothing. The forests surrounding our village would provide us with fuel. At dawn, we would sing and dance when a baby was born. At the end of the day we would cry and mourn when the

5. Tom

funeral drum announced the passing of some beloved neighbour.

At Market Square, I had boarded a packed bus for Southville. Just like in the old days, it had been a job to get on it. Somehow people seemed to know who was an ex-combatant and who was not. As an ex-comb, you were half revered and half feared. It helped. People made way for you. A young man in his twenties offered me a window seat. Maybe that was the only time anybody was ever going to treat me like a hero. So I thanked him and took the seat. It made me feel old but I didn't care.

On the way, I decided I would go to Mara's house first and invite her home, to 434 Sunningdale Road. I couldn't wait to see her. My body was aching for her. I wanted to know if she had decided to have our baby or not. If she had not, it wouldn't matter too much. On the other hand if she had the baby, it was going to blow my mind to discover that I was the father of a seven-year old boy or girl. I wanted to be with my twin brother Tom and his girlfriend, Emma. I hoped they were now married and might even have a niece or nephew for me. I wanted us to have an enormous meal and some drinks. I wanted to wake up late, very late, and find Mara by my side in bed.

I got off the bus at the business centre. It was strange finding myself back in Southville. The place was teeming with people. I hadn't seen so many buses, old bangers, scooters and bicycles weaving through such crowded streets for a very long time. I saw quite a number of new buildings. Among them I could identify three new supermarkets, a nightclub and a couple of off-licences. All the roads in and around the shopping centre were now tarred. As I made my way towards Mara's home, the houses seemed smaller than I remembered them. Here and there, a house had been extended, fenced or re-painted but otherwise nothing much had changed.

Every garden seemed now to have a mango, guava or some other fruit tree. There are more people in Southville now, I thought. The township was still very colourful. Compared to the countryside I had seen earlier on my way from the assembly point, the city had been untouched by the war. There was a glaring difference between the city and the rural areas where people had really suffered and the land was devastated.

As I came up to the house, I cursed myself for forgetting to buy something for Max and Joey. Before I could knock on the door, a short middle-aged man opened it. He greeted me cordially and asked me if he could help. I asked for Jerry. The man told me the house had been sold to him some five years before. He knew Jerry, as everybody did, but he didn't know where he lived now. He suggested that if I went to Discount Supermarket, someone there might be able to help me as Jerry owned it. I thanked him and turned back to the supermarket. I felt deflated at the prospect of not being able to see Mara that evening. But maybe Tom now had a car or could get hold of one.

At the supermarket, I was directed to the manager who turned out to be very arrogant. He refused to tell me anything about Jerry or how I could get in touch

5. Tom

with him or his family. He put me in a very bad mood. I warned him that if he behaved the same way with me next time, I was going to put a bullet through his thick skull. I threw him a blank which I had in my pocket and started walking out. He came running and told me to wait while he wrote the addresses of Jerry's home and office. He even gave me the telephone numbers. I looked for a phone booth. The first one wasn't working. The second one had been vandalised. At the third, there was a queue of about twelve people. I so badly wanted to see Mara that I went back to Jerry's supermarket and asked my friend the manager if I could use the phone. He was very happy to oblige. He tried calling for me but the line was engaged for a long time. He offered me a cold beer while I waited. At last he got through. Some female voice told me Jerry was out and would be home late. I asked her if she was Selina. She surprised me by saying she didn't know anyone by that name. I reminded her that Selina was Jerry's wife. The shock. Jerry's wife had died six years before. I felt numb.

She knew nothing about Mara. She suggested I try to call Jerry the next day. My hands were shaking as I put the receiver down. Selina. She and I were always joking and laughing. As I walked out of the shop, I was overwhelmed by the thought that both Mara and Tom might be dead as well.

I hadn't gone far from the house before I started regretting coming out. No, it wasn't the heat. Wherever I tried to go, it seemed like the whole of Southville was out on the same street. People everywhere: kids, old people, men, women and babies. No, I didn't see their dark faces. Just wave after wave of bright and colourful clothing. The singing, cheering, hugging and dancing on the streets was euphoric. It made the air feel solid. I don't know why but I began to feel edgy and irritated. Why were they all so happy? What were they going to get out of the national celebrations? I didn't care about the celebrations. I didn't feel the world had just been born. I wished I was far away from these noisy and crowded streets. All I wanted to do was forget the war and everything that had happened in the last seven years.

Later that day I left my clothes in a locker at the railway station and went bar-crawling. I finally ran into a group of comrades, including Comrade Fara who had been in my detachment in the last months of the war. We all still had money and drank like fish. Almost all of them had jobs lined up, some in high positions. I couldn't understand it. I was brave enough to question it. I could not see how Comrade Fara, a man in his early twenties with no high school certificate, qualified to be such a high official in the Ministry of Foreign Affairs. My comrades laughed at me and told me that I was a fool. We had not spent all those years fighting and risking our lives to come and let other people make money and take decisions over us. That night, we all went to Comrade Fara's newly acquired house. It was a huge furnished house. He couldn't swim but had a swimming pool. Somebody complained of hunger. Comrade Fara took his Colt 45 and went to his chicken pen and shot a chicken which we roasted. I stayed four

5. Tom

days at Comrade Fara's house. I had convinced myself that it was better to get a job and earn some money than continue with studies.

I tried to see Jerry. Emma had told me he had an office on the corner of First Street and Fife Avenue but I had not imagined how big or how plush it would be. When I got out of the lift on the second floor, a heavy guard in a smart uniform was sitting at a desk behind a big glass door. He opened the door and asked if he could help me. I told him I was there to see Jerry. He told me to come another day.

I decided to do nothing further until I found out what had happened to Mara and Tom. On my next attempt, I tried to make an appointment with Jerry's secretary over the telephone but it was hopeless. For three days, the only time the phone actually rang was after hours, when there was obviously nobody in the office. The rest of the time, I found it perpetually engaged. I decided to go to the Ministry of the Interior. It was early but there were already many people in the waiting room of his office. I took my place in the queue and waited my turn. There were all kinds of people there.

The person just before me was a girl in a school uniform. She looked pregnant. Next to her was a blind old man. After him was a young man in a police uniform. He seemed to be with a woman who was breast feeding a baby. For twenty minutes after my arrival, the queue did not advance at all. There were twenty-four people ahead of me and five had come in behind me.

125

After about two and a half hours, which I spent trying to guess what each individual had come to see Jerry about, my turn finally arrived. His secretary, a very civil woman, asked me to sit down and asked me how she could help me. I gave my name and told her I wanted to see Jerry. Politely, she explained to me that he would need to know what I wanted to see him about. I apologised to her for bringing a domestic issue to the office but that was the one place I could easily get hold of the man. I told her I was there to discuss Mara, Jerry's sister-in-law. She gave me an understanding smile and immediately went into an inner office. When she came back, she informed me that he was very busy but had asked that I write to him about the problem. To soften my disappointment, the secretary suggested I should try and visit him at home since it was a personal subject. I thanked her and left. Out of desperation, I did write to Jerry but, as I had expected, I never heard from him. All that was a mere three years ago.

I tried to see him at his house. He had a high security brick wall. The top of the wall was crowned with broken glass and razor wire. I can still see the heavy solid-steel gate being opened by an armed guard. Another guard was waiting inside. I was terrified when a pack of mean looking dogs appeared. One of the guards at the door asked me for my name and what I wanted to see Jerry about. I told him my name but informed him that the subject of my discussion with Jerry was private. With that, he left for the main house, came back and simply told me that Jerry did not know who I was and that he was not going to see me.

So I never managed to see the inside of Jerry's house. Jerry had forgotten me. As I walked away I felt hot – from humiliation. How could I start blaming Jerry for saying that he didn't know me? To him, I was a stranger. I had gone to his house without an invitation or an appointment. But that was exactly it. If I had really thought about it at the time, I am sure I would have realised that Jerry simply didn't want to see me. But instead I took it all at face value. I did not ask myself why, since he claimed he didn't know me, Jerry had not been curious enough to find out who I was and what I wanted. In his position, most people would have been inquisitive. I should have wondered why he had not tried to find out how I knew him. On the way back to Southville I began to suspect that the guard had not told Jerry about my visit at all. I refused to accept that Jerry could have dismissed me like that. I felt bitter and disappointed.

6. PETE

Tell me why she is walking if she can fly? How do you know she is walking and not flying? Well, you think you are a genius, tell me if she is walking or flying. She is still too far for me to see. If I go on sweating like this, I am going to faint.

Man, you think you have got problems. Look at that peasant woman. How does she do that? Two babies strapped on her back! That is just one load. She is also balancing a huge bundle on her head. She is carrying a heavy basket in her left hand! The free right hand swings back and forth, propelling her forward. I hate to think how far she has come. Must be going to the city to visit her husband. The children must be twins. Bet the husband hasn't seen the children since they were born. So she is taking them to him so that he can see them. The things we do for love.

Here now, we are approaching each other. Sweat is pouring down her young face. If she is not in her teens, she must be in her early twenties but she is already ageing. Lord, she is smiling. This is a very respectful greeting. She thinks I don't look well. I tell her it's

Tsiga

just the heat and not to worry. Her kind eyes are not convinced. She takes out an old bottle half full of water from her basket and offers me a drink. I tell her to keep it for the children and ask her how far she has come and how far she is going. She is coming from Murewa and going to the city. I had guessed right about the twins and her husband. I feel guilty talking to her while she has all that on her. She insists I take a sip or two.

Gratefully, I take the bottle and take one gulp, and then another. I hear her apologise because the water is warm. I thank her as I give her back the bottle. A violent storm is gathering in my stomach. I barely hear her telling me to have some more. I try to wave her on her way but it's too late. Every drop of the water that went down cleans my guts and erupts out through my mouth and nose. When it's all over, I am embarrassed and feel ungrateful. Her tender eyes look at me full of worry.

She puts her bundle and basket down, but not the twins, and attends to me. I feel awful but I try to reassure her that I am all right. I urge her to continue her journey. But she takes me by the arm and leads me to the shade of a tree a few paces away from the road. She has got her basket in the other hand. She sits me down and breaks open a watermelon from the basket. She gives it all to me. I try to protest but she won't hear of sharing it.

She can see I don't know how to express my gratitude. She smiles and respectfully takes leave of me. I watch her walk to the road, pick up her bundle and continue along the road. I eat my melon and look at

6. Pete

her from time to time. I begin to feel so good, I smile. I finish the melon and thank her even though I know she can't hear me. I watch her descend into a dip in the road. When she comes out to climb the other side of the dip, she is already changing into a fly. At the top, she turns into a fully fledged fly and disappears beyond the horizon. Now I wonder if she was real or just something out of my imagination. I know I am feeling very sleepy and can't keep my eyes open. I lie down and ask myself why I used to pretend that I didn't eat watermelon. Before sleep finally conquers me, I make a silent prayer for the soul of that saintly woman.

I dream about an old man who claims to be Mara's father. I realise the man is in fact Pete. He tells me if I want to find her I should go with him to his house.

I overslept but God knows I needed the rest. When I wake up, I re-read Mara's letter. The image of Pete as an old man haunts me. The sun is going down and it's now a little cooler. Time I pressed on if I am to arrive at the farm before dark. Should be able to do it now. I can feel some energy in my body.

The evening of the day Tom returned to the city, Pete suddenly showed up at Mutoko. I was surprised to see him as I thought he was in the city Anyway, I thought he had heard about father's death and had come for the funeral. When he came inside the house, in the light, I was shocked to see how bruised and swollen his face was. His left arm was in a sling. We sat down and I asked him what had happened. He told me the police had come to the campus and arrested three student leaders for political agitation. The students had then tried to organise a march to the central police station where their leaders were being held to demand their release. The colonial authorities had responded by sending in the riot police to break up the march. Their way of doing this was to attack the students. In the clashes that followed, several students had been injured and many had been arrested. It had not yet been officially announced but the colonial government had decided to close down the university for a time. They wanted to weed out all the student activists.

According to Pete, the political situation in the city was very tense. A group of students including Pete had escaped from the campus and made their way to Southville. After a secret meeting with Jerry and other officials of the Youth Wing of the Liberation Front, the students had been directed to head for the liberated zone to join the Liberation Front Army. For security reasons, they had thought it best to travel separately or in small groups.

Pete had managed to travel from the city to Mutoko by catching several different buses and walking through forests to avoid police roadblocks. Pete told me that the security forces were sweeping through our whole area rounding up all young able-bodied men in an all out effort to stop them from going to join the Liberation Front Army. He warned me that I would certainly end up in jail if I tried to return to the city. I told him I would wait until I made contact with my brother Tom whom I was now very worried about.

Pete suggested that we travel to the liberated zone together because if I stayed at Mutoko, I was going

6. Pete

to be caught in the police dragnet and would end up in jail. I told him I couldn't do that for a number of reasons. First of all I was not as brave as he was, nor was I committed to the cause as much as he and others were. I wasn't going to play the hero.

My immediate concern was the whereabouts of my brother. If he had made it to the city, I wanted to join him as soon as possible. If he was missing, I was going to look for him even if it meant going to jail. In any case I couldn't just disappear like that without telling Tom where I was going. What would he think?

My father had just died and I had stayed behind to make arrangements with somebody to take care of our home and our livestock, which I was yet to do. I reminded Pete that my father had sacrificed a lot for me to get to university. I wasn't going to quit now, just a few months before my degree. I told him Mara was pregnant and I had no intention of abandoning her and the baby just like that. Pete knew better than to argue with me. We had grown up together at Mutoko. As toddlers, we had scratched each other in the face and thrown sand in the other's eyes when our mothers, who were sisters, tried to get us to play together. Later, we had gone out herding in the same group of village boys. We had started school in the same year in the same class and took turns at the top of our classes.

During puberty, we had been sexually liberated by the same older girl in the same week. For some time, we even became the best of friends until Geraldine, the most beautiful girl in our school, came between us. She had rejected both of us because we were too young for her. After she left school and married one of our teachers at the age of seventeen, Pete and I had become friends again. But we were not as close as we had been before. At university, coming from the same village brought us closer once more but by then we had different passions. For Pete, politics was everything. For me, life had many other colours.

We sat down for our evening meal and continued talking. Pete told me he was leaving Mutoko for the eastern liberated zone the next day. He was sure the security forces would arrive in the village within a day or two. Most of the people being arrested were first tortured for information and then sent to detention camps if they were innocent. Those that could be charged were charged and went to jail. A number had died during interrogation. Once in jail or in detention he didn't see how any young man was going to be released until the war was over. Did I really think that they would let me out and let me go to the university to complete my degree? A year or so ago, that might have been possible. But now, things had deteriorated and the regime had become more oppressive. If I was arrested, I would not be able to get in touch with Tom, Mara or anybody else for that matter. Pete thought that the more of us there were to go and fight, the sooner we would overcome the colonial regime. We would all have a better future, including the child I was going to have with Mara.

Pete went on chipping away at my arguments until the early hours of the morning. More out of fear than conviction, I ended up agreeing to go to the liberated

6. Pete

zone with him. We agreed to start off the following evening. From the moment I agreed to go with him, Pete made himself the leader and took most of the decisions for us. To get to the mountains where everybody knew the Liberation Front Army ruled, we had to head east. Pete had decided, for security reasons, that for the first two nights, we should travel at night and sleep during the day.

That way, we minimised the risk of running into the security forces or meeting inquisitive people. Once in the liberated zone, we would travel during the day. He had also decided that we should travel light so we could travel faster. If at some point we had to run, obviously we would run better without luggage. I asked Pete what we would wear if we didn't even carry a few clothes.

He assured me that once we got to the liberated zone, the Liberation Front would provide us with food, clothes and some money. He also told me there would be no problem about food on the way. Once the peasants understood that we were on our way to join the Liberation Front Army, they would feed us and give us shelter. Pete thought the journey would take us no more than three days. I assumed he knew what he was talking about and accepted all this. So we set off with nothing except a roast chicken, a loaf of bread and some water.

As we walked out of the village, Pete was in very high spirits. I was not. I was thinking about Tom and Mara. I persuaded myself that Tom got back to the city without too much trouble. He was all right and was going to work. He was waiting for my call in two days time. He didn't know that it wasn't going to come. On the third day he would start worrying and decide to wait another day or so before making inquiries. Mara, with tears in her eyes, would go and see him and beg him to take her to Mutoko. She would think I was sick and alone and helpless. Tom would urge her to wait another day or two. She would inform Tom that she was going to check if I was in any of the city hospitals. She would also go to the central police station to find out if, by chance, I had been arrested. Tom would get up very early the next morning and go to Market Square terminus to send a letter with the bus conductor to Aunt Irene, Pete's mother, to ask if she had any kind of news about me. In the evening after work, he would go and wait for the bus conductor at the terminus.

The conductor would give him the reply from Aunt Irene in which she would say she didn't know where I was. However, she would add that Pete too had disappeared. That way, he would figure out that I had gone to join the liberation struggle. He would be mad with me for not telling him a thing about it but he would at least know where I was. He would try to find a way of telling Mara about it but he would put off telling her. When he had finally gathered enough courage to tell Mara, she would just laugh and not believe him. But for her, days would stretch into weeks, weeks into months, without any kind of news from me. What would she do next? I had no idea.

6. Pete

That first night, we travelled through an area we both knew well. We took care to avoid villages and main roads. We knew most of the people in this area and they knew us. We didn't want anybody asking us questions. The only problem we had was with barking dogs in one or two villages. But they never came anywhere near us nor did they do enough to attract attention to us. We stopped once, after midnight, for a short rest. Dawn saw us a long way from Mutoko. Just before sunrise we arrived at a seventeenth century stone-built fort and decided to spend the day there, hiding and resting.

Neither of us had ever been beyond this fort. From the overgrowth in and around the fort, nobody had been there for quite some time. It therefore seemed a secure place. It was musty and damp but I didn't care because I was exhausted. I was more tired than hungry and went to sleep right away. As is usual when I sleep during the day, I had a terrible nightmare. When I woke up late afternoon, Pete was snoring away. I ate and drank some water before going outside to look around. I noticed a thick column of smoke rising in the distance.

When I heard the sound of gunfire, I decided to wake up Pete. He thought that it seemed more likely that it was the "security forces" terrorising a village than a battle between them and the Liberation Front Army. Later, at dusk, when we set off again, Pete insisted we pass through the smouldering village. He assured me it would be quite safe as the security forces would never dare stay outside their bases after dark. He was

Tsiga

right. We found an old couple and many dead people, mostly children and women. I was horrified but Pete behaved as though he had seen it all before. He started lecturing me about why we should fight the colonial regime but I shut him up. The old couple advised us to leave the corpses alone as some of them had been booby-trapped. We walked them to the next village where they knew people. We were fed and given good directions towards the mountains in the liberated zone.

It was a moonless and chilly night. I had never travelled through a thick forest at night before. It was a scary experience, especially the silence. I saw the shapes of lions, leopards and all kinds of other dangerous animals in the dark forest. I found solace in silently cursing Pete for putting me through all this. I made up my mind that this was the last time I would travel at night. We marched for three hours before we stopped to rest on top of a hill. We descended the hill into another thick forest. A short way from the base of the hill, we heard the roar of a lion not that far from where we were. Pete collapsed to the ground with fear while I raced up a nearby tree. When I looked back, Pete was up and climbing another tree. The lion went on roaring for what seemed like forever. We remained in our trees until after sunrise. We walked on until we came to a rocky mountain range. It was now getting hot and we were tired but we agreed that the best place for us to stop and get some rest was somewhere up the mountain. It was a hard climb.

Halfway up the side of the mountain, we found a shallow cave and decided to camp there. We ate and

6. Pete

Pete went to sleep right away. Although I was very tired, I couldn't sleep. Looking around, I realised we were in one of the most beautiful parts of the country. I wandered off, higher, to the mountain top. With an aerial view of the east, it was a great feeling to gaze at chains of hazy, jagged mountain ranges. Here and there, I could see gushing mountain streams. Below, beautiful deep valleys and lush rolling downs dividing one mountain range from another. Apart from a column of smoke to the west, I saw no other sign of life. I felt so peaceful and serene that I asked myself why I couldn't live there forever. It didn't make any kind of sense that I was on my way to participate in the war. All I could think of was that it would be wonderful if, one day, I could bring Mara and our child here.

I was disturbed from my thoughts by Pete calling out my name. I was annoyed with him for howling out my name like that. I suspected that he thought I had gone and left him alone. But when I went down to him, he was very excited to show me some rock paintings he had just discovered. They were very old and showed a group of hunters killing an antelope. Outside, the sun was too hot so we sat in the cave and talked a little. Eventually, I fell asleep. When I woke up just before nightfall, we discussed and agreed to spend the night in the cave and continue our journey in daytime the next morning.

That night was long and cold. I was glad when the sun rose. I had spent most of the night thinking about whether to go back home and face all the consequences or go and be trained to fight whole-heartedly. I wanted to be resolute about what I was doing. I wanted to stop resenting Pete for my decision to go with him. I needed to feel that I was completely responsible for any decisions I made. By morning, I had concluded that I was caught up between two bad choices but the better one was to go and fight. At least that would enable me to retain some control over my life whereas if I were in jail someone else would be running my life.

I wasn't sure what would actually happen once we got to the liberated zone but I knew I was going to be trained and then sent to fight. I was going to fight to win. If I got killed or defeated, that would represent a betrayal of Tom, Mara and our baby. Having my mind made up, I felt much better. Even Pete noticed my changed mood.

We ate the last of our food and drank the last drop of the water before climbing up the mountain to go down the other side. It was hard going because it was very hot. When we had put the mountain behind us, we came to a river with cool clear water. We drank some water and then decided to bathe. I enjoyed a long swim in the river. It felt as though we were the only human beings in the world. While I swam, Pete lay in the sun to dry himself. A large flock of birds suddenly fluttered away from a nearby tree and frightened him out of his wits. He jumped up and took off, stark naked, like a gazelle. He looked so funny I laughed my lungs out. I was still laughing when he walked back with an embarrassed grin on his face. I teased him about failing to give me any warning and of abandoning me to be devoured by wild beasts. We got dressed and hunted for wild fruit before we continued with our journey.

The next two days were extremely difficult because we had no food, water was scarce and we were no longer certain that we were going in the right direction. We had left the mountainous region behind and were now travelling through a vast area of savannah grassland. We found no wild fruit here. We crossed no rivers or streams. We depended on dirty animal watering-holes for water. All we had to do to locate a watering-hole was to look out for a herd of buffalo or for giraffes. If we had some weapon, we could have killed a duiker, eland or sable antelope.

The animals were not frightened by us at all although we passed within a few metres of them. However, one afternoon, we did have to flee from a white rhino and its young one. The presence of large numbers of different animals in this savannah grassland area meant this was a rich hunting ground for lions. For this reason, we were eager to get out of the area as soon as possible. We were hungry and weak and couldn't walk very fast so we had to spend one night in this area. I was afraid of lions. Pete was more concerned about pythons. So we agreed to scale and spend the night on top of one of the wind-sculptured rock formations that littered the plain. It was a most uncomfortable night.

The next morning, we started off early, and covered a lot of ground before it was too hot. We spent the whole day without food or water. Tired, hungry and thirsty, we finally stumbled on a small village in the middle of nowhere soon after sunset. Although the poor people of the village gave us water, food and shelter, they regarded us with suspicion. Intending to continue with our journey the next morning, we asked for directions to the nearest Liberation Front Army base.

But the chief of the village informed us that we could not leave the village. He told us that a detachment of the Liberation Front Army would come and fetch us. On asking him when they would come for us, the chief looked irritated and ignored us. He informed us that if we were going to be fed, we should also contribute by doing some work in the fields and around the village. This seemed fair enough and we agreed to it.

For five days, we worked in the fields with the peasants. It was hard for us city dwellers but we got used to it. Pete thought we were wasting our time in the village. Working in the fields was not what was going to liberate the country. He suggested that we slip away and continue to the liberated zone. So on the night of our sixth day in the village, we tried to escape when we thought that everybody had gone to sleep. Barely a hundred metres out of the village, we were surrounded by five menacing young men armed with axes and spears. Not a word was spoken. I was quaking with fear. Pete was drenched in sweat They led us back to our hut. Until Commander Fara and his men arrived nine days later, we ate, worked and slept under guard.

When Commander Fara and his twenty-five heavily armed men arrived the village brought out the best it had. They were treated like heroes. A goat and some chickens were slaughtered. Some beer materialised

6. Pete

from somewhere. The daughters of the village placed themselves at his service. Pete and I were briefly presented, like booty, before being dismissed. The commander's party lasted all night. Pete and I were woken up at dawn with an advance party of fifteen soldiers. We did not have time to say goodbye to our hosts in the village. We marched all day long, with one short stop to eat and drink. Pete and I, as newcomers to the ranks of the Liberation Front Army, were treated with derision, especially since we could not walk as fast as the veterans.

I resented being made to feel more like a prisoner than a volunteer. There was no spirit of camaraderie. The only pleasant moments were when one of the soldiers asked us something about the city, like if a certain kind of beer was still on sale. After forty-five kilometres of marching we arrived at Camp 7 at dusk. We were placed in a make-shift barrack with eighty other people. We slept on the bare ground with no blankets. This didn't bother me because I was too tired to care.

I woke up the next morning to discover a whole new world. Camp 7 was located high up, on the side of a mountain bordered by a tropical forest to the north and a bare granite hill to the south. The camp itself was a shanty town hidden in a tropical forest, obviously for security reasons. It was a depressing collection of mud huts, old tents, cardboard shacks and large thatch sheds. Just looking at the hundreds of children, women, men and old people in the camp, it was obvious that this was a refugee camp and not a military base.

I was very upset by this discovery. I had not left home to come here to be a refugee. Anyway, what were teenagers and young people in their twenties doing in a refugee camp? Why were they not in a training camp? And all those babies. Why were there so many babies in this refugee camp? Surely people were not here to raise families? In all, I later learned, there were about four thousand people in the camp. There was so much misery written all over people's faces, I wanted to leave the place as soon as I could but I didn't know how it was done. It was at Camp 7 that I learned to wait, wait and wait.

The day began with assembly at five o'clock in the morning. First there was a roll call to see if anybody was missing. I was told people did try to escape from the misery of the camp but very few actually managed to get away. The majority were caught by the armed camp security men. They were then thrown into a damp underground dungeon where they were left for a few days without food. I was warned that trying to escape was just not worth it. Roll call was followed by physical exercises, accompanied by liberation songs and morale raising Liberation Front slogans. Normally this lasted until seven. If there was enough maize meal, we gathered in the cooking area, which was in the centre of the camp, for our rations of porridge. Of course nobody ever had enough, even though some got more than others. If there was no breakfast, which was quite often, we reported to our work-groups where sometimes we were given work, such as cleaning the camp or repairing one of the structures.

But there was never enough work for everybody. When that was over, the majority of the people were required to leave the camp for the surrounding woodlands, in case the camp was bombed by settler regime aircraft. But there were defined limits beyond which people were not allowed to go. If one went beyond these limits, one was bound to be met by the tough camp security men. This measure was meant to stop people from the camp going to the nearest villages to beg or steal food or clothes. Day in, day out, people tried to kill time as best they could but it wasn't easy. A small number tried to study without books, paper or pens.

Most sat or slept and day-dreamed about the future. Others would wash their clothes in the river, without soap, and bathe while waiting for their clothes to dry in the sun. The whole camp depended on the river for drinking water and cooking water as well. There was always a thick film of dirt floating on top of the river water. I was told there were twelve camps like ours in the area, situated all along the river. Six of them were upstream from us.

The sick were allowed to stay in camp. There was always a sizeable number of sick people considering the conditions in the camp. Diseases varied from malaria, fever, diarrhoea, high blood pressure, severe bilharzia and other diseases to infected wounds. We had some medical officers but they simply did not have the medicine. The little medicine that the Liberation Front managed to obtain was, naturally, for our men at the battlefront.

We had toilets in the camp but with so many people, it was hard to keep them clean. The toilets would get so filthy that virtually nobody dared use them. Instead, people relieved themselves behind bushes and other places around the camp. This, of course, invited flies which helped spread disease. At least three children and one or two adults died in the camp every week.

Usually, we had one main meal a day. We stood in the same long lines to receive our rations. We didn't sit down because the meals were so meagre. Everyone was perpetually hungry. After the meal we had political education before retiring to bed. Pete and I spent our first week sleeping on the floor without a blanket or any kind of covering. Some of our new friends showed us how to make beds from sticks. Everybody had a bed like that. It was another week before we were offered hessian sacking for our blankets.

One thing I enjoyed at the camp was the crisp mountain air. The other was the breath-taking views of the surrounding country with its dramatic mountain ranges, steep cliffs and green wooded valleys. I had a lot of time to think things over. I sincerely regretted having been misled by Pete but the reality was that I was here. I had to make the best out of the situation. The only consolation was that I was not alone.

Nineteen days after arriving at the camp, I was one of the people called for questioning. Commander Fara and two other comrades served as the panel in a grass-

6. Pete

hut. Here is the end of this limbo, I thought, as I entered the hut.

"Your name, comrade?"

I told him

"Age?"

"Nineteen."

"Where did you live before you came here?"

"Southville Township, in the city."

"You came here directly from the city?"

"No, Sir." I explained about father's death.

"Here we don't address each other with imperialist terms like Sir. It's comrade. OK?

"I didn't know, comrade."

"What were you doing before you came here? Were you working, unemployed, studying or something else?"

"I was a second year student at the university, comrade."

"Why did you leave your studies?" I was a little surprised by the question.

"To join the armed struggle."

"You are telling us you left your studies with just one year to go and a bright future in front of you just to join the liberation struggle?"

"A lot of other people have done that."

"Comrade, I asked you a question. You answer it!"

"Yes, comrade."

"Yes what?"

"I left my studies to come here."

"He is lying," remarked one of the comrades. It made me angry but I tried to control my temper.

"Why, should I lie?"

"Here we ask the questions and you answer them. Do you understand, professor?"

"To me it's very clear this man is a spy. He was sent here by the security forces to infiltrate the organisation."

I was choking with anger. I wanted to tell them to let me go home and continue my studies but I knew that would be a foolish thing to say.

"Who is Sergeant – ?"

"I am afraid I don't know anybody by that name."

They all looked at each other.

"He is afraid he doesn't know anybody by that name! Liar!"

"Nobody in your family works in the security forces?"

"No. Nobody."

"Not even an uncle or a cousin."

"No. Not even an uncle or cousin."

Commander Fara looked at his two comrades and wondered if they had any further questions they wanted to put to me. They shook their heads negatively. The commander stood up and extended his hand towards me. I didn't understand the meaning of this and I am certain it showed on my face.

"Congratulations, comrade. You have passed your test with flying colours. I am sorry for appearing to be rude but that is the way the test is designed."

I wanted to cry with relief but instead I shook my head and just smiled. The other two comrades also shook my hand and welcomed me into the Liberation

6. Pete

Front Army. While I was waiting for the rest of the people I was to train with, I would work in the education department as a teacher.

I was invited to ask any questions I liked, any at all. All I wanted to know was how soon the military training would begin. It was Commander Fara who answered me.

"To be honest with you, count on several weeks. Believe me, this is not how we normally work. We are having more recruits than we anticipated. This has thrown all our logistics into a mess. We know how you all feel but we're working on it. Now, one final thing, if you have no more questions that is, everybody in the Liberation Front Army has to have a nom de guerre for a number of reasons, but above all to protect our families from victimisation. If you have a suitable name, tell us – otherwise we shall have to give you one."

I couldn't think of a name just like that.

"All right, from now, you are Comrade Che."

With that, I had enlisted in the Liberation Front Army.

The truck that was meant to take us from Camp 7 to the military training camp arrived very late in the afternoon because it had broken down somewhere on the road. Our group, seventy-five strong, had waited for it since seven o'clock that morning. Most of us had given up any hope of leaving that day. When it finally arrived, the driver did not even turn the engine off. We scrambled up the sides of the open truck and shouted our farewells to the comrades remaining behind and soon we were on our way. We were all in high spirits because at last we were on our way somewhere.

But our happiness was short-lived. The comrade driving the truck was a maniac. He sped through the bush track as though he was in a safari rally. We were thrown forward and backward and from side to side. An hour after we left Camp 7, darkness fell and he went on driving the same way. None of us recruits knew how far the training camp was. I asked one of our four armed escorts how far the camp was. All he could be bothered to tell me was that we would be there soon. Soon didn't come until some three and a half hours later when most of us were half dead.

Finally the truck stopped in a small wood surrounded by hills on the south and the west and bound by a river which ran from the north to the east. I thought it was because, at last, it had occurred to the driver that we all needed to relieve ourselves. When our escorts ordered us off the truck and told us we had arrived at our destination, I was certain it was another unpleasant joke. We were in the middle of nowhere. There was not a single sign of life. There were no buildings, not even a simple camp-fire. No barking dog in the distance, nothing. Only an owl hooted .

Moaning and groaning, we got down from the truck and waited for new instructions. The truck turned round and sped off into the darkness. We were left with our four escorts. After a while we were told to assemble and sit down. This was where our training camp was going to be, one of our escorts told us.

6. Pete

Food, medical supplies and other essentials were going to arrive the next day. We were going to build toilets and underground store rooms and secure our camp by digging trenches. Those of us who would pass the medical examination would undergo a body building course before the military training proper could begin. We would be told more about our programme by the Base Commander and our instructors when they arrived. He then invited us to ask questions. One man wanted to know where we were going to sleep that night without any blankets. We all murmured support for the question. The escorts laughed at us. We were then told that as soldiers of the Liberation Front Army, we would never have a permanent base until the war was won.

Habits like eating at fixed hours, sleeping long hours or at specific places with the luxury of blankets or bathing regularly had to be broken. We were at the camp to train as fighters. We were told to start the life of soldiers of the revolution that same night. We were dismissed. That night Pete and I slept on the ground under a tree.

It took three weeks for the training camp to start running as planned. Only nine recruits failed their medical examination and were taken away from the camp. We were very well fed, compared to meals at Camp 7. Working around the camp helped build up our muscles. When the Base Commander and his team of instructors arrived they found us ready to begin training. A routine was soon established. Our basic day began at four in the morning with a breakfast of tea and maize porridge.

At the beginning, this was followed by body building exercises like running on the spot, drills, obstacle racing and so on. Initially, we used sticks instead of real weapons in training. Later, of course, we learned how to handle a variety of weapons. Except for very short breaks, we would not rest until noon. We sometimes had game meat and vegetables for lunch. We would have another half an hour's rest before starting the political lessons. At the front, we were going to depend for our own survival on the local population. The enemy often poisoned water sources so we were taught to always check with local people if water was safe to drink. A number of comrades had lost their lives ignoring this lesson.

We were not going to march and fight all over the country carrying huge reserves of food. We were going to depend on local people for our daily needs. It was on the people that we were going to rely for information about enemy movements and therefore our security. Once or twice we might get away with harassing or intimidating the people but in the long run, we would be the losers. We therefore had to treat people with a great deal of respect. We had to win their hearts and minds. We should discuss their problems with them and make them see that the war was their war. We had to make them feel we were their children, brothers or sisters. If they didn't know what the war was about, it was our duty to explain it to them patiently. Later we were taught propaganda methods.

6. Pete

It was eleven long months before I was finally called up. I was very happy to leave the camp but not without a certain amount of sorrow. I had made a few friends whom I knew I would miss. During those months, I changed a lot. I no longer had regrets about anything. University? Hell, most people in the world had never seen the door of a university. If I was special, was it going to university that made me better than most people in the world? No, I didn't think so. Somewhere in the world, day and night, babies were being born and men and women were dying. Who was I to be afraid of death? To be scared of dying? Love? Who lived for love alone? You have to be someone, you have to be there alive in order to love. Well, Mara was there and I was here fighting to survive, fighting to live. I learned my love with Mara was in one dimension of time and I was completely in another. She could have been there with me to fight in the war and love but she wasn't. One day, maybe one day after the war…

Because Pete was good at yapping, they had made him into a political commissar. He could sing too and that was supposed to make him a better commissar. Once, after a battle he came to raise the morale of our detachment. Unfortunately for him, we had been in an ill- advised battle the day before. Friends and comrades had been killed by real bullets. We were sad and tired. And there stood Pete, telling us that the spirits of our ancestors were there and had been invoked to protect us from death at the hands of the colonial settlers' security forces. He went on preaching so much he got excited until a little soldier who had just lost a twin brother in the battle sprang up and sprayed the air above Pete's head with a whole cartridge of bullets. Pete really did shit in his pants. He left the same night.

Two days later, we were ambushed in a different position and we brought down a French-built helicopter gunship but not before one of its bullets penetrated my right foot. That is how I got this limp. For several weeks, I kept on thinking: that bullet could have gone through my head and I could be dead. I thought about death and decided no one lived forever. Nobody. But why should anybody pump iron into me? Hell, why!? I wasn't going to take a hard time like that. I was going to shoot better. I was going to fight to survive. Another way of thinking about it was I was dead and could not die twice. I fought no better or worse than my comrades but I became so careless I don't know why I am not dead. I got used to the war. Nobody fought with the thought that the war would come to an end. We got used to winning some battles and losing others. We learned to prize our dead and draw inspiration from them.

Water, food, shelter and all that became less important than winning battles and keeping alive. We all seemed to understand that without discussion. I can tell you we were no longer fighting for politics. We were simply fighting the enemy. Our survival did not depend on the politics but on ourselves.

Pete had grown bigger. He came to us again when they were trying to break us up and integrate us into other detachments and we were resisting. Pete preached to us how we were going to take over the

6. Pete

settlers' children, wives, homes, jobs and businesses. But that wasn't what we wanted. We told him what we wanted. We told him we wanted clean water for us and our children. We told him we wanted our traditional food. We told him we were ready for development. We told him the lot. This time nobody shot over his head. He found it easy to lie to us by telling us that because we were the only real freedom fighters what we thought and decided would be the rule of our land. He told us the people were going to have to respect our wishes.

One day we were in the middle of a battle I thought would never end. The next day, the war was suddenly over. Most of us were surprised and then we even felt rather disappointed because we had thought we would march into the city with the flag of the Liberation Front Army flying. We also heard the news that our chief of staff, the man who had always given us the orders, had mysteriously died. But the order to cease fire had come from the commander in chief and had to be obeyed. To be perfectly frank, the war ended badly for me and a lot of my friends. It was all very orderly. We were all counted into assembly points. This didn't feel like a revolution.

Was I safe without my AK47? Would I go back to the university and finish my degree or would it be better for me to look for a job? It was questions and questions to which I had no answers all the way back to the city.

7. FATHER

I have carefully thought about all this. My mind is at peace. My conscience is clear. In the last day or two, every time I think about it, I feel a thrill – a mixture of fear and excitement. No, far from it, I am not scared.

For me, this is a reassuring feeling. Usually I never do go through with anything important unless I feel this nervous tension. I have pictured myself killing the vile creature in so many different ways, I don't care whether it is going to be a bloody messy job or a clean cut so long as he ends up dead. Only after that shall I worry about my feelings as a human being. Killing him, after all, might give me a reason to live like a good man.

Morally, I might have been feeling better if I thought I could surrender myself to the police after killing him. I am certain I do not wish to do that. To be punished for Jerry's death suggests I am the criminal. But I know he is the criminal. I am quite determined to be punished for anything else, even for a crime I have never committed rather than to be sent to jail for his death. Nobody deserves to be punished for his death.

No one believes that a beggar like me can be smart. Pity is what they rain on me and my kind. The judgment comes easy: he couldn't cope. He crossed the line. He is finished. He is sub-human. He is beyond redemption. In other words, he is dead. End of interest.

If, eventually, I am arrested, my life in prison – in a purely physical sense – would be a lot better than this life in the street. You couldn't have any idea of how many times I have been humiliated in this heartless city merely for asking for a glass of water – until I discovered the water taps in public toilets. At least in prison they give you clean water to drink. I have never been in prison, but I am certain prisoners have at least one square meal a day. Here on the street, now and again, I have to do battle with a dog over a bone from what you call a rubbish bin. There is another freedom I would happily lose. With a shave, a haircut, a shower and a prison uniform, I am sure I would look more like my twenty-seven years than the old man I see reflected in the shop windows. The only showers I have known these last three years are those from the sky. There have been days and nights in the cold or rain when I have been tempted to follow the examples of other homeless people and commit a petty crime in order to be hauled to the shelter of a prison cell or to inflict a wound on myself and spend a day or two in some hospital. Why, with a bunk-bed and a blanket my now perpetually red eyes should regain their brown colour again. If not, I trust the prison doctor would be able to do something about them. In prison, I wouldn't have to wonder how to spend the day. My fear of imprison-

7. Father

ment has always been based on not being able to have sex – but what sexual life have I had in these last four years? In the privacy of a prison cell one can at least masturbate, which is next to impossible on the street.

The criminal justice system has at least one serious flaw; it knows how to punish my body but not my mind. What I do with my mind in prison is entirely my own business. I won't allow them to imprison my brain. All this does not mean I am prepared to go to prison. Just a contingency plan.

When I told Mara that father was ill and I had to go to Mutoko, she suggested we go together. I didn't think it was a good idea. First of all, her absence home would compound the problems with Jerry who still didn't know that she was pregnant. It would be quite difficult for Selina to take the children to and from school and be at the shop. Although Mara herself was pregnant, she was still going to school. I saw no reason why she should miss classes. There was very little she could do to help in Mutoko. I knew she was in a very delicate state of mind and needed my support. So I tried to be very tactful, but Mara was insistent. It took Tom's intervention to convince her that her coming with me would cause more problems than it solved. Although she finally agreed, I knew that she was very anguished about it.

Before I left, Tom suggested that I should try and persuade father to come back to the city with me if he was strong enough to travel. Of course, I was to take him to hospital if I found him in a serious condition. I promised to send Tom a message about father's condition.

The morning was already hot and sticky when we arrived at Mbare. The place was remarkable for its variety of odours and its filth. It stank of everything from rotting vegetables to stale tobacco and urine. Summer or winter, the ground was always damp, if not muddy. No wonder there are mosquitoes all year round. All kinds of characters were found at Mbare. Rural innocents, young and old arrived from their villages. Workers migrated between the city and their rural homes at month ends through Mbare. It also had the biggest market in the city. Honest stallholders and peddlers of stolen goods did business. Business thrived too for gangs, pickpockets, pimps and prostitutes who gave it to anybody who could pay standing up. For me, Mbare was the worst part of going home or coming back to the city. Anything could happen. I wanted Mara to leave before my bus departed but she wouldn't hear of it. We kissed and hugged until Manu, a cousin who worked as a bus conductor and had reserved a seat for me, came and told me it was time to go.

I kissed Mara goodbye and got on the bus. I took my seat and the bus started moving. Mara was still standing where I left her. Despite the tears in her eyes, she looked radiant in her white frock in the morning sunshine. She looked really beautiful. I waved at her. She waved back. I kept my eyes on her until she disappeared from view. That was the last time I saw Mara.

7. Father

The two hundred kilometre journey from the city to Mutoko usually took about three hours by bus, so I expected to be home by lunch-time. But Manu told me things had changed a lot since I was last home. He told me to keep my cool and be very patient if I wanted to get home. He told me to keep my mouth shut as there were detectives on the bus and warned me not to involve myself in other passengers' problems.

At the Grange, just outside the city, our bus joined a queue of other vehicles at a police road-block. It took nearly an hour before our turn came. Everyone had to get off the bus with his or her identity card. While police officers with sniffer-dogs searched the bus and examined the luggage, other officers double checked our identity cards and asked each passenger where he or she was going and why. Two young men without identity cards were promptly arrested and shoved into a police van. The rest of us were allowed to continue. I was surprised by the number of military vehicles, full of soldiers, travelling in both directions.

Sixty kilometres away, at Murewa, we came to another road-block. The officers here were particularly callous and brutal. Instead of asking us to get off the bus and check our identity cards, they boarded the bus. One of them asked a very soft-spoken young man where he was going. The young man told the officer that he was going to Mutoko. For some reason or other, the officers didn't hear the reply. Instead of just asking the young man to repeat his answer, the officer whacked him in the face. An elderly woman issued an involuntary pained cry. The officers turned their attention on her. They roughed her up and insulted her. She pleaded with them to leave her alone but the policemen became very excited and started dragging her out of the bus. This treatment of the old lady outraged many of us on the bus but only one young man was brave enough to go to her defence. After a struggle, two men and the old lady were taken off the bus and we were allowed to proceed.

At the Mutoko road-block, all the passengers had to get off the bus, reclaim their baggage and wait for a thorough inspection. One set of officers checked identity cards and asked questions. A rather good-looking young woman with a baby was arrested for no reason other than that she was nervous. As far as the officers were concerned, she was nervous because she had something to hide. There were no female officers, so male officers did the body searches on women passengers as well. There was a man with a brand new radio in his suitcase. The officers asked him where he had got it. He told them the name of the shop and how much he had paid. Clearly he was telling the truth. They wanted to see the receipt for it but he had not bothered to keep it. They told him they thought it might be stolen property and took it away from him. We spent almost two hours at Mutoko before we were allowed to continue.

Soon after Mutoko, the reality that a war was raging in the country became evident. We saw burnt out army trucks. Here and there we saw the ruins of a bombed school or an abandoned village. At Sassa where Pete's mother used to live, the shopping centre and the entire

7. Father

village had been reduced to rubble. Manu told me that a battle had actually been fought there and many of the villagers had been killed in crossfire. Those who had survived had either been rounded up by the security forces and placed in "protected villages" or had fled to the liberated zone and sought protection under the Liberation Front Army. Manu informed me that the security forces, wanting to flush out the Liberation Front Army and to deprive them of hiding places, had cut or burnt down the forests. I had never seen so much devastation.

Tom had asked father to come and live with us in the city several times but I felt guilty that we had not tried harder. I resolved to take him back with me no matter how much he protested. The bus finally got to Mutoko at about three in the afternoon. When I arrived home, father was in a more serious condition than I had imagined. It frightened me to see him so emaciated. It was apparent that he should be in hospital but there was nothing I could do until the next day. The first thing I had to do was go out and fetch some water from the borehole, a kilometre away.

While the food was cooking, I gave father a dry bath and got him into some clean clothes. I fed him and tried to make him as comfortable as I could. I didn't know what was the matter with him nor could he tell me. All I could see was that he was very weak. Neither of us could sleep. We spent a very bad night. I sat and watched him breathing with difficulty until dawn when he finally fell asleep. I too soon dozed off. When I woke up, I was surprised to see father actually sitting up.

He was in high spirits and cheerfully wished me good morning. He looked so much better. I told him I had come to take him to the city or to Mutoko Hospital.

"Take me to hospital? Can't you see that it's too late for that?"

"You are looking a lot better than you were when I arrived yesterday. A day or two in hospital and you will be on your feet."

"I am not going to any hospital and that is that. Do we understand each other?" he said in a firm cold voice.

I knew he meant it and felt powerless as I nodded agreement.

"I don't want to die in hospital surrounded by strangers."

"Father, you are ill but you are not going to die. At least not now. So please stop talking about dying. Tom and I want you to come and live with us in the city."

"I wish your brother was here."

"I can send a message and ask him to come."

"No, my son. It's too late."

The tone of his voice and the expression on his face just didn't go along with his words. He certainly didn't look like a man who would die before Tom could arrive from the city.

"Don't talk like that, father. You still have at least another twenty years ahead of you. I am going to send a message to Tom and he will be here tomorrow or the day after."

7. Father

"I don't want you to bother your brother until I am gone. But there are some things I want you to tell him from me. Tell him that I want things to remain as good as they have been all these years between you and him. I am very proud of how close we three have been since your mother's death. Our home, the fields, the sheep, goats, pigs, chickens and everything else I leave to Tom and you. Do you hear me?"

"Yes, I hear you, father."

"Good. And tell your brother I want him to look after you until the day you marry. The last thing he will do is pay your bride price. After that, you will be on your own. I know you are both good boys. All I wish is for the two of you to settle down in your jobs, look after each other and your families. You understand me?"

I was getting very confused. True I had never seen anybody dying but I had always imagined them in terrible agony. I thought they physically struggled against death. If father had been delirious, I could understand him talking like that but he wasn't.

"You know why I didn't want to get married again after your mother died?"

"No, I don't know, father."

"Two reasons. I am still in love with your mother. I would never have been fair to another woman. I would have always compared her to Janet. That would never have been right. That's one reason why I didn't want to do it. My second reason was you and Tom. I knew that once I got married again and had other children, we would be pushed apart. No matter how good the woman would be, I knew it would happen. I couldn't bear the thought of a wedge between us..."

Without being really conscious of it, father fell into a nostalgic mood. His memory took him back to his youth. He told me how he and his friend Tendai spent three weeks travelling to Cape Town, the city of their youthful dreams and almost starved to death on the way. By the time they got there, they didn't have a cent between them. Somehow, they survived. After months, they managed to get jobs. Once the money started coming in, they spent it on elegant clothes, girls and a good time. Dancing was their main thing. He couldn't remember how many girls they had gone out with over the years. Home was too far away to be remembered. One day, Tendai met and fell in love with this really high-class girl. He soon got her pregnant. She loved him and wanted to marry him.

But for Tendai she wasn't the type of girl he could take home because he couldn't see her fitting into rural life. Father tried to persuade him to marry her anyway since they were not likely to go home soon but Tendai went further and decided to get rid of her altogether. The girl had a whole clan of brothers and when they heard the shame brought on their sister, they went for Tendai. The police said he had thirty-six stab wounds, each one fatal. Barely ten people came to the funeral. Five weeks later, after seventeen years in Cape Town, father took the train home.

"I met your mother two days after I arrived. Within a few months we were married. The talkers said it wouldn't last because I wasn't serious. Time proved them wrong. We settled and soon you and your brother were on the way. The rest you know."

I had never heard him express himself so freely and with so much passion before. Although he seemed almost happy, I thought talking so much was exhausting him. I eased him down on the pillow but he went on talking. He looked a man in real agony.

"I am not going anywhere. I don't want to die in some strange place. I'm not afraid. I'm looking forward to being with your mother again."

I believed him and tears streamed down my face. I held him very tight as though it would stop life ebbing away from his frail body. He submitted like a tired child.

"I love you and Tom very much."

"I know, father. I know. We love you too."

"I couldn't wish for better sons".

He looked straight into my eyes and then smiled.

"Shall I sing you a song?"

I knew he was going to sing my favourite lullaby. It seemed funny somehow. I laughed.

"I think it's going to take a lot of energy out of you but I would love it if you sang me just one verse and the refrain."

He started singing. It was awful. He was squeaking more than singing. After the refrain, to my dismay, he went into the second verse. But his voice was weak and fading. By the last words of the refrain, I could hardly hear the words. After the song, he died. I sat there alone with him until I had no more tears left to shed.

Tsiga

In those hard days before independence, people didn't go to funerals to mourn the dead but to cadge a meal and maybe enjoy a drink if the dead person's family could afford it. People even joked about it: if you want a good crowd at your funeral, make sure you leave plenty of food and drink. Although father had been something of a recluse and refused to have intimate friends, he was generally well liked.

Tom arrived two days after father's death. I had taken no decision on feeding the hundreds of people camped at our home. It was the poor peasants themselves who brought whatever little food and drink they had. We buried father the same afternoon. But people from outlying villages were still arriving. There had been neither food nor drink to entice them. We were very touched by this and decided to throw a feast in memory of our father. People ate, drank and danced day and night for three days.

Tom had to hurry back to his job in the city. He asked me to stay for a few days. We couldn't go and just abandon all the people at our home. I had to find someone to look after our home, the land and our animals until we decided what we were going to do with them. I was missing Mara badly. I had asked Tom to bring her to the funeral but he had not been able to contact her or Selina. So she didn't know that father had died and I wouldn't be back in town for a few more days. Tom was going to see her and tell her what had happened as soon as he got back.

8. MARA

I remember it was a Friday. My last lecture finished at twelve. I had gone back to my room and packed my weekend bag. I was in a hurry because I wanted to catch the bus into town. I soon joined one of several groups of other students taking the short walk from the campus to the bus stop. It was hot and everybody was complaining about the heat. When the bus came, it was too full. My cousin Pete and his friend arrived and we waited for the next bus together. We all waited a long time but no bus came. The three of us agreed that it was better to start walking into town than to stand and roast in the sun. We started off and tried to hitch a lift as we walked along.

A few hundred metres down the road, an old car stopped for us. It turned out the driver had stopped because he knew Pete. We piled in and he drove on. When I looked at him, I thought I recognised the face of the driver but I couldn't place it. Clearly they knew one another very well because they immediately fell into an animated conversation. No introductions were made. They were talking politics so I didn't bother to listen.

When they dropped me off at the corner of Second Street and Union Avenue, I was still trying to work out where I had seen the driver before but I just couldn't remember. Eventually, I remembered that I had seen his photograph in the paper. But his name continued to elude me. From bits of their discussion, I finally realised this was Jerry, a well-known member of the Liberation Front. I had listened to him address a rally once and had been very impressed by his speech. I felt very honoured being given a lift by him. Ten minutes or so later, they dropped me in town. I wished everyone a happy weekend and parted. I was thirsty and decided to have a soft drink before I caught the next bus to Southville. It was when I was paying for the drink that I realised I didn't have the key to 434 Sunningdale Road where my brother Tom lived. I wasn't going to go all the way back to the university for it. I decided to go to the hospital where Tom's partner, Emma was a student nurse. I would borrow her keys. It wasn't far. I walked there. As usual, Emma was very happy to see me. She agreed to lend me her keys and gave me some money to buy some food for that evening. I made my way to the bus stop for the bus to Southville. There were five or six people at the bus stop as I approached but it was the girl in a simple white frock who caught my eye.

She had a very shapely body, I thought to myself as I crossed the road. I was only a few paces behind her. She had a slender neck, nice legs and the colour of her skin was closer to ebony than gold. When I got to the bus stop, I was eager to look at her face but she was in the middle of the queue and I was at the back.

8. Mara

Waiting for the bus, I paced up and down, hoping to have a glimpse of her face but all I could see was her back, her black sandals and her handbag. Her hair was short and neatly combed back. I was thinking of a way of attracting her attention when the bus arrived. We all boarded and the bus roared on. I had to see her face, I resolved. I watched her as she walked all the way to an empty seat near the back of the bus. I finally had my wish when she turned and sat down.

Her deep misty brown eyes and mine met for an instant. It was I who looked away as an intense thrill raced up my spine. Instead of sitting next to her, I found a seat on the other side of the aisle from her. I felt moist all over. I sat down and shamelessly fixed my eyes on her. I didn't care a damn what anybody else on the bus thought of me. No girl had ever made me lose my calm like that before. As I listened to my heart thudding, I made up my mind that wherever she was going to get off the bus, I was going to be right behind her. The bus stopped. I wasn't going to chicken out now, so I followed her off the bus.

I found myself walking a few paces behind her. I had a feeling she knew I was following. I didn't know what I was doing. I was afraid to talk to her. With my hands in my pocket to hide how nervous I was, I followed her. Gradually, I caught up with her. She gave me a sideways glance.

"Hi," I heard myself croak.

It wasn't my voice at all. I felt like running away.

"Hello," she replied in a very pleasant, soft voice.

I had always thought I was good at chatting up girls but now I did not know what to say next.

"What's your name?" I asked, my voice still not under control.

It took her a few moments to answer.

"Why do you want to know my name?" she asked, giving me the slightest of glances.

"Why! So that I can get to know you," I said and began to feel my voice was returning to normal.

Again, she took her time.

"I don't want to know people whom I don't know," she said and I laughed.

She actually turned her head and looked at me with a smile.

"What's so funny?" she asked, looking away.

"Did you hear what you said just now?" I asked.

"This is a funny conversation," she remarked.

" Yes it is, because every time I ask a question, you answer by asking me another question."

"I didn't mean it that way."

"Oh, how did you mean it then?"

"Never mind. You ask too many questions."

"OK. Now are you going to tell me your name?"

"Another question! My name is Mara," she told me.

That did it. I began to feel relaxed.

"Mara… Mara," I muttered to myself.

She looked at me with curiosity.

"Are you trying to remember another Mara?"

"No, no. I was just trying to think if there could be a better name for you than Mara."

8. Mara

"So you don't like my name?" she asked in a teasing voice.

"On the contrary," I protested, "no other name could go better with your looks."

She chuckled, looking at me.

"Flattery won't get you anywhere. Anyway, you haven't told me your name."

I felt another thrill. She was interested. At least she wanted to know my name. To me that was something.

"That, I shall tell you next time we meet," I replied.

"Cheat!" she cried cheerfully, "There isn't going to be a next time."

"If there isn't going to be a next time, why do you want to know my name?"

"Listen," she said in a serious voice, " thank you for walking with me. I am home now. Maybe we shall run into each other again. Take care."

I felt my inside sinking.

"I would really like to see you again."

"What for?"

"To talk and maybe go to the cinema?"

"I am sorry, I can't."

I stopped. She walked a few paces more before she turned round, stopped and looked at me. There were no tears on my face but she could see I was really sad.

"Don't be like that. We met today. We shall meet again," she told me, as though she was addressing a little boy.

I didn't say a word. She took a couple of steps towards me and looked straight into my eyes.

"Please, don't be like that," she pleaded.

"Can we meet tomorrow?"
"No," she said, firmly.
"Day after?"
"No."
"Well, when then?"
"I don't know. Why do we have to arrange it? Maybe we will just run into each other some day."
"Mara…?"
"Maybe next week."
"I can't wait until next week."

We looked at each other in silence for a few moments.

"You are putting pressure on me. It's not good. I can't think. I must go now. Tell me your name."

"And then we can meet tomorrow?"

"Maybe Sunday afternoon."

I told her.

"I have had to bleed it out of you but that is a genuinely nice name."

"Flattery won't get you anywhere," I said, and we both laughed.

Before we parted, we agreed to meet at two o'clock on Sunday afternoon outside a café called "The In Place" which was at the shopping centre. I felt on top of the world. I completely forgot to do the shopping Emma had asked me to do until I got to the house and then I had to go back to the shops.

Sunday didn't come soon enough for me. I arrived at half-past one and hung around. Most people were dressed in their Sunday best but I didn't feel too out of place in a pair of jeans, a T-shirt, a sports jacket and my

8. Mara

new black shoes. There were a lot of families window-shopping or out just for a stroll. The cafés and the beer hall were full of people. There was never much to do on a Sunday in Southville unless there was a football match or a political rally. Shortly before two, I went to wait for Mara near "The In Place." She was late. I began to wonder if she would show up. I was thinking of all the reasons why she might not come when she arrived.

Mara looked like a princess. Her plaited hair was decorated with multicoloured Indian beads, which matched her necklace. She wore just a touch of make-up. Her embroidered pale yellow dress fitted her body perfectly. I was tickled by the idea that she had made all these efforts for our date. It also did my ego a lot of good to be seen with her. I did see a few heads turn as we stood there, discussing what to do with our afternoon.

Tom had suggested that I invite her home but I had told him I didn't think she would accept. My idea had been to take her to the cinema and then have a drink in some quiet café. Seeing how excited I was about Mara, Tom had given me some extra cash. She turned down my ideas of going to a movie, going to an afternoon disco or going to a rather smart café in town. What did she want to do, I asked. She told me she would love to go for a walk in Baxter's Wood. I wondered why such a simple idea had not occurred to me. We left the crowded shopping centre for the more peaceful Baxter's Wood.

"How do you spend your time?" I asked.

"I get up very early in the morning, clean the house, prepare breakfast for my brother-in-law, my sister, their two children and myself before going to school. On my way from school, I pick up the boys from the crèche and go to the grocery store where my sister works. Usually, I help my sister at the shop before taking the boys home and starting to make supper. I bath the boys, feed them and play with them until their parents come home. We eat. I wash up and then do my homework or read before going to bed. So you see, I lead a very exciting life," she told me.

"And at weekends?"

"Usually, I am very busy. The boys are at home. The week's laundry has to be done and ironed. The house has to have a thorough clean up. There are always visitors to feed."

"You mean you never go out?" I asked.

"Oh, I do. I am out with you now, aren't I? Generally, I can do what I like on Saturday and Sunday afternoons."

"What sort of things do you do when you have free time?"

"What is this? An interrogation?"

She said she liked films. She liked reading and had read almost everything that was worth reading in her school library. Her sister thought she spent too much money on books. She enjoyed long walks. She liked all kinds of music but was no good at dancing. If I wanted to go dancing, I was never to ask her to come with me. I promised I wouldn't.

8. Mara

Mara was born in Southville. Her father was a motor mechanic and her mother was a school teacher. She had an elder sister, Selina. When Mara was eleven, she lost her mother in a car accident. The girls were then brought up by their father. At the age of eighteen, Selina fell in love and got married. Mara continued to live with her father until Selina's first baby, Max arrived. Then she went to stay with Selina and Jerry, her husband, to help with the baby. She stayed and stayed until she ended up living with them. Mara's father re-married but the marriage didn't last. Soon after the end of the marriage, he gave up his job and disappeared. They hadn't seen him since.

From what she told me, I was able to work out that she was about nineteen years old. She was doing her sixth form and was almost certain to go on to university the following year. She wanted to study English because she wanted to be a writer. As we walked past Southville cemetery, she told me her mother was buried there. It was so comfortable being with her. I was beginning to feel as though I had known her a long time. I wanted to tell her that I was in love with her but I decided it would be better if I waited until we knew each other better. But in a quiet spot in the wood, I made up my mind, I was going to try and kiss her even though it was our first date. For that, I had to wait because we were still some way from the wood.

Mara thought it was my turn to tell her everything about myself. I said I had nothing interesting to tell.

"You do seem to have a problem in talking about yourself. Why is that?"

Tsiga

'No, I don't have a problem talking about myself. I am not used to it, that's all."

"Well, if we are going to be friends, you had better get used to it. You know I think I have seen you somewhere before."

"I like that. I hope it was in your dreams."

I explained that I was born in a village near Mutoko. I told her my father still lived there and that my mother died giving birth to Tom, my twin brother, and me. We had been brought up in Mutoko by our aunt. We came to live in Southville with our father to continue our schooling when we were about nine. Our father never re-married. He taught us to do everything for ourselves. After his fifth form, Tom had decided to train as a photographer. He was so good that as soon as he finished training he was offered a job on a daily newspaper where he was still working. I went on to do my sixth form at Southville High before going to university where I was studying physics. Father was retired and worked as a peasant farmer, growing cotton.

As we came to the edge of Baxter's Wood, without thinking about it, I took her hand into mine. She didn't react positively or negatively but I got the feeling that she would prefer it if I let go. After a very short time, I did. She turned, looked at me and gave me a small smile.

"How old are your nephews?" I asked.

"Max is five and Joey is three. They are great kids. They are very demanding but they are a lot of fun to be with."

8. Mara

"Good. I hope I shall meet them one day. Your sister works in a grocery store. What does her husband do?"

"No. My sister and her husband run a grocery store. She does more of the work than he does. Jerry spends most of his time working as the organising secretary of the Southville branch of the Liberation Front."

Something clicked in my head. I suddenly remembered that I had seen the driver who had given Pete and me a lift behind the counter in a grocery facing the Southville market. I also remembered that Tom had taken a picture of him where he had been described as the organising secretary of the Southville branch.

"That's interesting. He had just given me a lift from the university when I met you last Friday."

"Everybody seems to know Jerry. Are you interested in politics?"

"I support the cause but I am not an activist. And you?"

"Of course, I support the cause too but some characters in the Front put me off."

"Like who?"

"Never mind. I really should not have said that."

There was no doubt in my mind that Jerry was one of the characters she had in mind. I didn't want to annoy her by pursuing the subject. We were silent for a while.

"How well do you know Jerry?" Mara asked me.

"I only know him by sight. That's all. Why?"

"No, I thought you might be friends. He has a lot of friends at the university."

"I am not one of them."

It became very clear to me that Mara didn't like Jerry. I wasn't going to ask her why. Not now anyway.

By now, we were deep into the wood. I had been there a number of times before but it was soon apparent that Mara knew it better than I did. Like an excited little girl, she led me to a small rock by the river that ran through the wood. There we sat down and continued talking. She was relaxed and looked radiant but what undid me was the discovery that she had a formidable intellect. I think because it was our first time out together, we didn't go deeply into any one subject but I felt there was nothing I could not discuss with her. We discussed a little bit of politics, touched on economics and sociology but we spent most of our time talking about films and books.

"You must live in a very intellectual household. Do you discuss things with Jerry?"

She gave a scornful laugh.

"I don't know what your image of Jerry is but believe me, because I have had to live with him, he is a typical Dr Jekyll and Mr Hyde. I don't think he is politically sound but he is very popular. Sometimes people are like sheep. They just follow. I just don't see how he can be such a good politician when at home all he does is terrorise the children, brutalise his wife and he sees me as nothing but a sexual object he would like to screw given half a chance."

We sat in silence for a while.

Finally I put my hands around her neck and started kissing her. For a moment, she didn't react. Then she embraced me. It was magic. We kissed and cuddled a

8. Mara

long time until she warned me not to go too far. When we stood up, the sun was setting in a clear sky. She took my hand and led me out of the wood a different way. We walked in silence. I picked her a few flowers on the way and gave her a small bunch. We walked back to the township teasing each other and laughing. At the cemetery gate, she stopped and asked me if I wanted to go in and see her mother's grave. We went in and Mara swept all round the grave before putting the flowers near the headstone.

When we walked out of the cemetery, we discovered a riot had broken out. We were told that people were protesting against the arrest of the man who had been knocked down by a police car. The police station had been burnt down. Police vehicles had been overturned and set alight.

Barricades had been erected on the roads in and out of Southville. The smell of burning tyres and a black cloud of smoke hung over the township. We had to evade a number of running battles between the police and the rioters. We finally got to Mara's house.

"I really wish I could invite you in, but if Jerry is home or comes later and finds you there, he would make life hell for the whole house for at least a week," she said at the gate.

"It's that bad, eh?"

"I am afraid so. As far as he is concerned, any man who comes to the house without his knowledge is Selina's lover. At nineteen, I am still too young to bring a boyfriend home, can you imagine? The last time I brought someone home he beat her very badly."

We agreed to meet at Charles' Bookshop the next Friday.

That is how Mara and I began.

No, Mara and I did not have the same brain in two different heads but we grew to read each other like one open book. We were very lucky. Neither of us ever suffered from emotional insecurity. There never was a need. She knew I loved her and I had no doubt that she too loved me.

It was Mara's idea. We pooled our small resources and bought a book a week. She enjoyed shopping around. I saw Mara a few more times before I invited her to meet Tom and Emma. Tom and Mara immediately liked each other. They discovered that they could talk to each other about anything. She asked him to teach her chess. They agreed to lend each other books. Between Mara and Emma, it was a different tune. Politely, they went round and round each other but found no common ground. There was no animosity. Just the difference between a lightweight and a heavyweight. Later, on the way home, Mara asked me if Tom was really in love with Emma or was there something else to it. I had wondered too but I decided to play the devil's advocate.

"Why? You don't think she is good enough for him?"

"I didn't say that."

"Well, what did you mean?"

"I know I shouldn't have said that. I am sorry."

I saw Mara almost every weekend. We usually met at Tom's house but sometimes she came to visit me at

8. Mara

the university. When there was a good film, we met in town and went to the cinema. Mara liked to sit down and discuss a film in all its aspects after seeing it. We would analyse the film, scene by scene.

One Saturday Mara invited me home for supper because Jerry was going to be away for the weekend on political business. She thought it was time I met her sister and the children. She told me Selina was very eager to meet me. Even though it was all innocent, I was a little nervous about being able to go to Jerry's house only because he wasn't there. Mara assured me that there would be no problem.

I arrived early so that I could have a little time with the children before they went to bed. Selina was still at the shop when I arrived. Mara introduced me to Max who was six and Joey who was four. At first the boys played shy but we soon became friends. We played cards and drew pictures while Mara cooked. By the time Selina arrived, the food was ready. Yes, Selina was very beautiful but no more so than Mara. She looked younger than I had imagined. We ate and then I played with the children again. I felt very honoured when they insisted I put them to bed. I told them a story until both of them fell asleep. Selina thought I would make an excellent father and I congratulated her for having wonderful children. I liked Selina for her sharp wit and her sense of humour. She made me spend most of the evening laughing.

Shortly before eleven o'clock, I thanked Selina and left. Mara walked me to the gate. We were kissing goodnight when a car drove up and stopped. Jerry had unexpectedly returned home. Mara was in a panic. I told her to pretend that I had not been in the house. She was worried Selina didn't know what was going on outside. We didn't have time to discuss it. Jerry came up to us. He was fuming. He ordered Mara to go into the house. She was worried he was going to hurt me. Suddenly, I took off. I wanted Jerry to chase me, hoping that it would give Mara time to warn Selina. He did chase me but it took no effort for me to lose him.

I was worried Mara wouldn't show up for our date at Tom's house the next day but she came – and on time. Jerry had slapped her a few times and warned her that the next time he saw her with her schoolboy lover, he was going to break every bone in both their bodies. Mara was just happy we had managed to keep Selina out of the incident because Jerry would have pulped her. I was worried the children might give the game away but Mara told me that the children were so frightened of him that they hardly ever said a word when he was around. I did go back to the house a few more times after that to enjoy the company of Selina and the children – but that was when Jerry was in jail for sedition.

We went back to the wood many times and made love. Our love-making was total. It was never sweaty or exhausting. On the contrary, it was liberating and energy-giving. Mara was not on the pill but her days were regular and reliable. We respected her cycle. We couldn't wait for Mara to come to the university so that we could see each other every day. That time never came.

8. Mara

Jerry, now out of prison and a well-respected nationalist, was becoming more and more hateful and brutal with his children, with Mara, and, above all, with his wife Selina. No one on the outside to which he was giving so much knew anything about his domestic life. His popularity continued to rise. Mara grew to hate him more.

About two years after we started dating, Mara got pregnant. We didn't know what to do. On some days, Mara would say she was going to have the baby no matter what and I would be totally against it. On other days, our positions would reverse. We didn't want anybody to know about it until we had made a final decision. Especially Selina and Tom. Mara entered her second month of pregnancy. We still couldn't make up our minds whether to have the baby or not. I began to feel that if there was going to be an abortion, we were leaving it a bit late. So I suggested that we should tell both Selina and Tom since in the end we couldn't do anything without their help.

Mara didn't agree. She thought we should learn to solve our own problems. She accused me of trying to panic her into a decision.

A few days later, a message came through that my father was ill back in our village. Tom was ready to go, but I offered to go instead because I had not been home for nearly two years. Father had come to town several times. I also thought it would do both Mara and myself good to be away from each other for a couple of days or so. She missed a class to see me off at the bus terminus.

Tsiga

There is the river. Cattle and goats are drinking there. The water is brown. I know up-river people are doing their laundry and bathing. The water is brown. That water is like poison but I am going to drink it just like the water we used to drink during the war. It is hot and I am getting tired. Time for a rest. I am going to sit under that figtree on the other side of the river for a while.

9. THE LETTER

Darling,

Everyday I wait for you because my intuition tells me you are somewhere, still alive. I don't know when or if you are ever going to see this letter. But if I am to live, I must write. I am afraid I write to give you a lot of bad news. I don't even know what to tell you first but I don't think it matters very much what I tell you first as long as I tell you everything.

We have had no communication since your father died, now twenty-two months ago. Please accept my deepest and heart-felt condolences. I wish I had been able to meet him. I only wish I had been there with you. I wish I had travelled with Tom when he went for the funeral. You know everything I wish.

Selina is dead. She was killed. I lost our baby. It was killed. Selina, my sister, your very good friend, is no more. And I no longer carry that baby we spent so much time talking about. The least of it all is that, day after day, I have been getting pulped to near-death, especially since Selina died, which is now just about a month ago. I have been taking it for the sake of Max and Joey. But after the latest calamity, I no longer can. He raped me, two days ago. I thought about it. I thought about it very seriously. But for you, life would not be worth living. I would trade the world for you.

The answer to most of your questions is: Jerry. When you didn't come back or write I suspected that like most young men, you had been caught in the gathering whirlwind of the war. I resolved to have our baby. No matter what happened to you, at least I would have that half of you. After you left, of course, Selina had to know. I told her. I also told her I didn't want to be a burden and I was going to leave. I would find some way to support the baby and myself until you got back but she didn't see it that way. She wanted to help.

She thought it right and proper that Jerry too should know. She suggested that I tell them both in a sort of formal way. I agreed. I agreed because I saw trouble for her if we didn't do it that way. After I told them, he turned into a smiling demon. Hadn't he fed me and clothed me? Hadn't he given me good shelter and an education? Hadn't he done this, that and everything for me. Selina made a mistake. She tried to pacify him.

All hell broke loose. He punched her into a coma and then took me on as I tried to restrain him. He knew where to punch. He knew what he was doing. He knew where to kick and he knew where to play his trampoline. The baby never had a chance. I miscarried right away. I didn't even go to the hospital. I didn't need to. What I needed was you. I wrote you a whole

9. The letter

book but I couldn't send it to some unknown place, c/o a tree, a mountain, a hill or a cave.

    I am waiting for you.
    With all my love,

                                       Mara

10. JERRY

To be honest, I am not sure I am feeling like myself. Something is not quite right with my mind. I am not ill or anything like that. I know I am thinking straight even though I feel a bit light-headed. Everything is as it usually is except nothing seems real. I don't know why I keep thinking that I am actually dead and my being is a spirit. As a spirit, I am nothing but a brain tissue floating high above the ground. It doesn't bother me that I can't see the whole little round world whether I am standing on the ground or sitting at infinity.

I know that if I move, I shall see less. I will let the world do the moving and stay there and watch.

In a way, I can't help feeling lucky to be dead. I can see parts of the whole wide world at a time but the world can't see me. How do I really know I am not dead?

No, since Twoboy was murdered last week, I have not been quite myself. The shock provoked both physical and mental strains. I have not eaten much in the last week or so. No appetite at all. The food just refuses to go down my throat. The amount of drinking I did between his death and the funeral could not have helped much either. Sleep. Well, I haven't really slept properly since they started killing homeless people a few weeks ago. Stay up at night and sleep during the day is the new rule of staying alive. Most homeless people now stay up at night and sleep in public places by day. My problem is that I can't sleep during the day. When I try, I always have the most terrible nightmares and wake-up drenched in sweat.

I am anxious about my meeting with Jerry. It must be anticipation. I am not sure how the meeting will go or if anything will come out of it. From time to time, I feel giddy. Not only do I think I know what is going to happen next, because it has happened before, but it all seems to have taken place a long time ago. No, I don't think there is anything wrong with my mind. No, I am not tired yet but it's beginning to feel quite warm. I must ask for some water to drink at the next village I come to. If I am offered some food, I am not going to say no, even if it means waiting for it.

The sun was setting and I was exhausted. I was hungry and thirsty. The first signpost I had seen announcing Capital Farm was now a good five kilometres behind me. I began to wonder if I had somehow missed the road to the farmhouse. No, I didn't think there had been any side road to my right. It couldn't be on the left because I could distinctly remember Emma saying it was on the right hand side of the road coming from the city. I was cursing myself for not getting more precise directions from her when an even bigger signpost appeared ahead of me. I was still too far to read it but I made up my mind that I would go no further

10. Jerry

along the main road for that day. If there was no turn-off road at the big signpost, I was going to turn back. I wished there was somebody I could ask.

The only people who passed by were in cars and buses. The last houses I had seen were six, maybe seven kilometres back. I felt very downhearted at the prospect of having to walk back all that way. All I could think of now was a drink of water. As I got nearer to the signpost, I was relieved to see that it also pointed to Capital Farm. I felt even better when I saw a well-used track leading off the main road. At least, I wasn't lost. But my joy didn't last long. As I looked up the track, I saw no sign of the farmhouse. Far away, I could see a hill where the track rose and then disappeared. My journey was far from over. I turned off the main road and followed the track.

I didn't know where the boundaries of the farm were but it seemed Jerry owned a small country. He had mountains and hills. He had valleys, streams and at least one river. On one side of the track, a young crop of tobacco stretched far back into a range of hills. I saw a large herd of cattle and a flock of sheep grazing on the other side of the small road. Further up, lush fields of maize spread out as far as the eye could see. It was no wonder Jerry could just give away seventy-five thousand dollars to people like Emma.

As the last rays of the sun were fading, I felt out of breath climbing a small hill. When I came to the top, the homestead and the compound where the farm workers lived just like in the colonial days came into view. I had only a kilometre or so, to get there. I stopped to catch my breath.

Half way down the hill, I suddenly felt a cold chill run up my spine. I shuddered. I realised I was afraid. I was shivering. I could not understand what was happening to me. No it wasn't Jerry that I was afraid of, that I was sure of. I thought I was falling ill. Then the wind started blowing behind me. I wanted to look back at the wind. Look at the wind? This was a sure sign that I was going crazy. If looked back, it really meant I had gone mad. The wind caught up with me. It caressed the back of my neck and blew through my hair, all the way into my brain. It was a warm soft wind with a heartbeat. I could clearly hear the sound of that heartbeat. It got louder and louder, I wanted to scream.

The heartbeat changed into the sound of footsteps. Maybe it was all in my head. Well, if I wasn't mad, I was dying. I tried to pull myself together. No, no, I was not mad. Tired yes, but not crazy. A lot of unconnected thought images flashed through my head. Then it was back to the footsteps.

They were there, unmistakable but I didn't want to look behind me. Finally, involuntarily, I stopped and turned round. And there stood this old man. He gave me a big smile. It was as if he knew me. Only four or five paces separated us. I was certain, by some power, he had been playing with my mind, for now I was myself again.

He looked about seventy. He was tall and looked very serene with his silver-grey hair. He came up to me and extended his big hand. I gave him mine. My

10. Jerry

hand seemed so little in his. There was a certain aura about him. His large, brown eyes seemed mystical to me. We exchanged a formal greeting and then introduced ourselves. He told me everybody called him Jim. He didn't bother to tell me his second name. I didn't think it right to ask.

"You are coming from the city?" he asked in such a cheerful voice that I was quite surprised.

I thought of lying but I found myself telling him the truth.

"Yes, I am coming from the city."

"Would you be visiting relatives on the farm?" he asked.

"Well, not exactly. I am actually looking for a job," I lied.

"I see," he said in an unconvinced voice.

We continued down the hill in silence. I was very uncomfortable with the silence. I asked him if he worked on the farm.

"Seventeen years, I have been here. I have seen three owners come, make their money and go. I feel part of the farm, so to speak," he said, laughed and slapped me on the shoulder. I didn't know it but he was lying to me.

"Surely you must be the head foreman by now," I said mechanically, because I was really wondering if I could kill him if I had to. He gave another short laugh and told me:

"No. We no longer have foremen, like in the old days. Now we have managers. I am what they call a section leader. I am just like any other worker except

I have the extra duty of checking who is present and who is absent. I note what time the workers begin work and when they finish."

"I hope they pay you according to your experience," I told him.

"I wish they did, my son. I would have my own farm by now. No, they pay us enough to eat and get up the next morning to go and work in the field. That is all. The wife works at the Big House to help make ends meet."

"Well, I would have thought that after Independence…"

He didn't let me finish.

"We all had great hope when Independence came. But now we know Independence is not for everybody. It's not enough to go round. I blame nobody. Don't misunderstand me, I am not complaining. I praise the spirits of my ancestors because, at least, I have got a job."

"You are right. You are right," I muttered, not knowing what else to say. No, I couldn't kill him. It was an absurd idea. I couldn't kill him even if those eyes were closed.

"Do you think there is a chance of a job?"

"There is no harm in asking the manager. Who knows, you might be lucky. Come home with me and have a drink of water. I'll take you to see the manager."

We entered the compound. Things were working out better than I had expected. But there were also some problems I had not foreseen.

10. Jerry

People wished the old man good evening and greeted me. He surprised me by introducing me as his son-in-law. We continued through the compound. It was a depressing place, a collection of shacks and huts all crowded together inside a grass fence. When I saw half-naked children with big round stomachs, images of Camp 7 rose in my mind. I followed the old man until we came to his huts. He invited me inside one of the huts. I sat down and realised how tired I was. He gave me some water in a big tin mug. I accepted it with two hands and gulped it all down. My stomach growled. The old man looked at me and asked me if I wanted some more. I shook my head and thanked him.

"You will stay with us tonight," he told me rather than asked me.

"It may not be necessary," I informed him.

He came and sat next to me. We remained silent for some moments. He wasn't looking at me but somehow I felt that he was slowly opening my skull. He wanted to get to my brain and watch it at work. I was determined not to be the one to break the silence. It didn't seem to bother him. Maybe he had finished boring into my mind but he broke the silence.

"I think I know you but I am not yet sure," he said, almost talking to himself.

"I thought I was your son-in-law," I reminded him.

"Can we leave that for the moment? I know you are not looking for a job. And if you are not looking for a job, I wonder why you are here. You are here on a secret mission. I have just been trying to work out what such a mission could be..."

I told myself whoever this old man was, he had extraordinary powers. But I wasn't going to let him change my life. The only way he could do that would be if he produced Mara there and then. That was one miracle I knew he couldn't perform. But I decided I would be completely honest with him.

"How did you know I was not looking for a job?" I asked him.

"People do not leave the city, no matter how hard life may be, and go in search of a job in a village or on a farm. Especially a bright looking young man like you. If you had said you were looking for a relative or a friend, I would have believed you."

He was right. I couldn't think of anything to say.

"I knew your name before you told me."

I looked at him sharply. Who was he? I was sure I had never seen him in my life before.

"In fact," he continued," I have been waiting for you."

"Please, just tell me who you are," I begged him.

He gave me one of his short laughs and said, "I am your guardian spirit."

I sighed and asked him, "What do you want from me?"

"To help you. That is all."

"How can you help me?"

"If you are looking for a job, it's time we went to see the manager. He lives behind the big house. I can't let you go alone because the guard won't let you in if you are by yourself. Even if you were to get in somehow, the dogs would savage you to death before anybody

10. Jerry

stopped them. No, I have not been seventeen years on this farm. This is my tenth month here. I have no wife working at the big house either. My wife died many years ago."

I stared at him as tears welled into my eyes. I threw my arms around him. We settled down for the night but, once the old man had gone to sleep, I crept outside and made my way to the big house.

The dogs were barking already. I wasn't close enough to silence them. I had no poisoned meat either. I decided not to worry until I was about five hundred metres from the house. It did no good. The closer I got the more the dogs barked. It took me some twenty minutes to find the right leaves and de-scent myself, as I had learned in the war. The dogs also helped me to establish that there was just one guard. He got so nervous that he kept on marching up and down in front of the gate under the floodlights. I could see, when I got closer that he was armed with an AK47.

I got on my knees and started crawling towards the gate. It took me a long time but at least the dogs had gone quiet. The man calmed down and resumed his seat by the gate. Right away, I knew he wasn't an ex-combatant. This made me feel good. I had no qualms about killing him. He wasn't my kind. I felt morally stronger as I crawled to within a few metres of him and took a deep breath. I had thought that my best bet was to distract him and let him shoot the air in the dark.

But another chance, a more peaceful chance presented itself at three metres. An owl hooted in the distance. Quietly, I shed my overcoat and felt like a guerrilla. The guard could kill me for the chance I was taking.

I had to wait and I waited for him to get tired and doze off. I crawled centimetre by centimetre as the man got into what I knew was his habit. For no reason at all I wanted to cough. I crawled one more arm's length. With my three fingers, I caressed the back of his neck and that was it. He didn't even fall. Stiff, he was dead.

It took me a long time, but in the end I had his clothes on and his gun in my hand. I knew about the dogs but I had no idea of who was inside or on the other side of the house for that matter. I pushed the gates wide open and sat on the dead guard's stool for about half an hour. I asked myself why the hell I was doing what I was doing.

It all seemed so funny that I laughed and started the dogs growling. Well, if they were going to threaten me now, I was going to simply pump iron into them – and anybody else who came into my view. With that decided, I saw it as the right time to take the house. I was ready for the dogs but not to risk making a noise. They came up to me in a friendly way and sniffed me. They appeared to be completely fooled.

I tried the doorknob. It didn't give. A sleepy middle-aged domestic woman came to the door.

I bent down to tie my shoelace.

"You have been drinking again, Simon!" she accused me as she opened the door.

10. Jerry

I made her sit down. When she realised she did not know me, the poor woman was scared out of her wits. I got as much information from her as I wanted about the household and about Jerry. She was so frightened she offered me everything from food to sex, as long as I didn't hurt her.

My stomach growled. I ordered her into the kitchen. With the help of the refrigerator in the kitchen and the pantry next door, she willingly made me an excellent meal.

"Are you married?" I asked her

"Yes, sir," she replied meekly.

"Children?"

"Yes, we have six."

"You are going to have seven if I accept your offer to sleep with you?"

"I don't mind. A child is a child and I love children but please don't kill me, sir."

"Stop calling me "sir". I don't like it. Call me comrade if you like."

"Oh, you are a comrade?"

"Don't worry. I didn't come here to kill you. I am not going to touch you either. I have nothing against you. You are married and have children and I hope you are happy – "

"No, I am not happy!"

"Why?"

"My husband. He used to be a policeman. He killed many comrades. He betrayed many comrades during the war."

"Ahaa, during the war. The war is over. We all forgive each other for what happened during the war."

"For everything!?"

I looked at her and remembered Mara. I wondered why I was being sentimental now.

Then Jerry walked into the kitchen. The gun was still steady in my hand but my palm was sweating. My eyes undressed Jerry. He was shit scared and looked like a wet chicken. I should have been feeling sorry for him by now but this man with the eyes of a snake had killed my unborn child. He had killed my little child whom I was going to give my mother's or my father's name. He had interfered with my love for Mara. I had not taken any chances. All I had to do was pull the trigger... And then what?

"How and when did you kill Mara?"

"I swear I didn't kill Mara. If she is dead, she is dead but I didn't kill her. Please, you must believe me."

My hand started sweating from holding the pistol for so long. I saw my child with Mara. She was a beautiful little girl with clear brown eyes who bore my mother's name. And this brute sitting before me had put her to sleep forever. It wasn't an accident. He had killed my little mother in Mara's womb. I had to kill him. All right, he denies killing Selina. He is not sorry she died. She was his wife. At least he has said nothing to indicate he is sorry. Who is he to have rights over other people's lives? I had a feeling he had not killed Mara but I was not happy with his explanation.

"I really don't want to kill you but you are such a dirty shit I think I have no choice."

10. Jerry

"I swear I didn't kill Mara. I am sure she is alive somewhere. I am prepared to spend my life and my money finding her."

Jerry's death was the lead story in all the newspapers. There were seven pages of a glowing obituary of "this outstanding citizen whom the whole nation will sorely miss." He was described as a hardworking patriot who had dedicated most of his life to the service of the people. He was a generous businessman who had given thousands of dollars to the poor and to the Liberation Front. The police had ruled out robbery as the motive for the senseless murder of the man most people believed would one day ascend to the presidency of the country. There was no mention of the dead guard.

Tsiga Nyika
Harare Central Prison

Works of W. Katiyo

A Son of the Soil – forthcoming at Books of Africa Ltd in April 2011 (First published by Longman, 1989, UK)
Going to Heaven – Longman 1979, UK